Books by TLW Savage

First Test Quartet

Alex Twice Abducted
Alex Terrified Hero
Alex Inner Voice
Alex and the Crystal of Jedh....Not published as of March 2019

Dark Universe Series

Alex Terrified Hero

TLW Savage

ISBN 9781094694283

Pronunciations

- A'idah – Ī ē duh

  Twelve year old girl from Northwest Pakistan, one of Alex's best friends and a member of his flock

- Amable – Ă muh bull

  The leader of the aliens abducting and training the Earthlings

- Coruscated – kor uh skāt ed

  Definition: *flashed or sparkled*

- Ekbal – ĕhk bal

  Twelve year old boy from southern India, a member of Alex's flock

- Gaahr – Gahr; simply ah with a hard g sound in front followed by the rrr sound

  A species of deem

- Gagugugul – Gah goo goo gull

  A Gaahr

- Gursha – Ger shuh

  The nurse for Alex's flock

- Haal - Hăl

  A dwarf

- Heyeze – Hī ēz

  An evil philosopher of the dolphins

- Hheilea – Hī lē uh

  A kimley fifteen year old girl

- Hhy Soaley – Hī sōl ē

  Hheilea in disguise as a boy

- Hymeron – Hī mer uhn

  Hheilea's brother

- Lepercaul – lĕp r call

  An alien specie

- Lillyputi – lĭl ē poo tē

  A wonderful desert, which is dangerously

  addictive for humans

- Maleky – Muh lĕk ē

  The most evil person in the galaxy

- Numbel – Nuhm bell

  A dwarf

- Osamu – ō săm oo: the oo is the same sound in boo

  A Japanese man and a member of Alex's flock

- Sabu – Să boo

  A snow leopard and a member of Alex's flock

- Skyler – skī ler

    A Blue Hyacinth Macaw and a member of Alex's flock

- Tierce – tirs; pronounced like tear plus a c sound like in pierce

    A fencing term referring to a type of block

- Twarbie – twăr bē

    A winkle female, who looks like she might be close to Alex's age

- Vapuc – vă pook

    The result of dark matter affecting a living creature to allow it to alter the laws of the universe

- Ytell – yuh tĕl

    A raptor, who is the leader of Alex's flock and the leader of the other raptors

- Zeghes –zā s
    A six month old dolphin who is a member of Alex's flock

DEDICATION

This book is dedicated to adventurers, romantics, and to all those people who are uncertain about their futures and maybe even scared about their futures. I hope this encourages them to be heroes in their own ways, maybe just to themselves. Also to my two daughters, Lynn and Laura, who first suggested I write stories for others to read and enjoy; and to my wonderful wife, Debbie, her forbearance through the years with my writing struggles allowed for the opportunity to continue.

This book wouldn't exist without the hard work and sincere efforts of Porsche Appleman, Laurie Rosin, Irene Roth Luvaul, Billy Melton, and Debbie Walker. The hundreds of hours you spent laboring with me were appreciated more than you'll ever know.

A very special thanks to a local author, Connie Jasperson, who has been there for me as a volunteer editor, fan, friend, and mentor.

I want to thank the many who helped me with the research. The Kalasha researcher, Wynne Maggi, for her invaluable help in understanding the Kalasha people. Lee Merrick of Alaska Falcons helped me to get the characterization of Ytell and the other alien raptors right. When I'm writing of the alien raptors I think of his beautiful Gyrfalcons.

Then there are the countless many who patiently listened to me talk about this story and read portions of it, just to give me feedback. You know who you are and I hope you find those who'll help you with your dreams.

Last, but not least is a great thanks to Laura for helping me finish this project.

What follows is for my fans. Two in particular come to mind: my first fan Judy, my little sister; and one of my most rabid fans, Porsche. Everyone, please read on, laugh, cry, gasp in terror, think, be amazed, fascinated, and enjoy.

CONTENTS

Chapter One
A Strange Thing Happens

A tall, gray hospital shouldered above the other buildings. Rows and rows of identical windows covered its sides. A raven on a tree branch looked through a window into one room, where a little boy begged his older cousin to eat a chicken leg. "Come on, Alex," he said. "You need to eat more."

Despondent, Alex looked away. "I'm not hungry and you better not let the nurse catch you with that chicken leg. She's a terror."

The little boy sprang forward, almost knocking over a glass of water. He waved the chicken at his cousin. "Dad fried it just the way you love it, and I snuck it in here just for you. I also brought something else in."

Alex frowned. He steadfastly looked away until a rustling sound yanked his eyes back. His cousin poured purple crystals into the water. A grin tugged at Alex's mouth as the water turned purple. Shaking his head, he said, "This is a bad idea. If that spills, the nurse will do more than yell."

"You told me this drink always makes you feel better. You need to eat and drink this to get well."

Alex turned his head away from the enticing smell and said bitterly, "I'm not getting better. Stop waving that under my nose and watch out for the glass."

"You promised me you wouldn't give up," the little blond boy said.

He's right, I did promise him. He was also right about the chicken. Alex used to love fried chicken. He didn't know what he loved anymore.

Thoughts pulled at Alex's attention like a whirlpool. The doctors in this hospital should've known what was wrong. They should've been able to heal him. He didn't want to die.

The picture the doctor had given him of a white-haireded gremlin caught Alex's eye. The doctor said to visualize something in you causing the problem and then you can fight it. *It's the doctor's fault I'm giving up.* Alex shook his head at the stupidity of the thought. *But it's not fair.* He remembered his dad's words from when his parents still lived. "When you're in a fight, don't hang on to anything except what helps you win." *I've got to stop being stupid.*

Alex looked back at his cousin. "I'll try that chicken leg."

His cousin, Sammy, lunged toward him holding the chicken leg. In the process, he bumped into the glass of water, and the food in his hand disappeared.

Alex stared, not comprehending. *Where did the chicken leg go? How...*

An excited Sammy said, "Alex! A raven just did magic." The words and laughter pulled Alex out of his confusion. He turned his blue eyes to look, and his mouth fell open in amazement. A raven flapped, pecking at the chicken leg hanging outside from the window pane. Tearing the chicken leg loose, the raven flew away with its booty, leaving a small piece of chicken skin stuck to the window. Alex stared at the window. *Magic? That's crazy. Uncle Nate would call it an unexplained phenomenon. My folks thought magic was evil. Could this be something God created? And could it heal me? I don't want to die.*

His cousin turned, and a premonition made Alex reach a thin arm out just as the little boy knocked the glass of water off his table. Alex snatched the glass out of the air. "I told you to be careful."

Just then the nurse came in and stood glaring at Alex, with her big fists on her hips. Alex stared at her in surprise while she said, "I hope you ate all the chicken Sammy brought in." She continued with, "You're going home. I'm going to miss you."

Chapter Two
Strange Things Happen

At home, Alex lay on his bed and stared at the ceiling. He thought about the series of unexplained events. He had started getting premonitions after his uncle remarried.

Alex sat bolt upright. *I started getting sick about then. Also, I've seen the grass growing impossibly fast by my aunt's window.* It was as if she'd brought something into their lives causing these strange things to happen. *I bet she's a blue-skinned alien and not a member of the Blue Fugate family from Tennessee. This could prove aliens exist.* He had never believed her story, even after he checked it out and found there really were blue skinned people.

The smell of food had been slowly getting his stomach's attention. One last thought crossed his mind before he gave into growing hunger *If only there was a way to get healed using whatever was causing these strange things.* Alex clutched at the tenuous hope, as he left his room to go eat. Seeing Sammy carefully balance three plates in one hand, as he set a glass on the table replaced Alex's agonizing over his own concerns with a worry for Sammy. Sammy wasn't supposed to help.

Alex's aunt entered the room from the opposite side, and snapped at Sammy, "What are you doing?"

His cousin looked up with a startled expression.

Alex opened his mouth to yell, "Look out," but it was too late. Sammy hit a glass, knocking it into the edge of a plate with a clear *ting*.

The glass flipped over the table's edge. Alex stopped breathing. The glass fell as if in slow motion. His guts clenched, and he lunged for the glass, even knowing it was beyond his reach. Suddenly, the glass stopped falling and hung in the air. Sammy grabbed it and almost dropped the plates.

Aunt Julia gasped, and her normally blue face turned darker, almost purple.

"Go to your room. There'll be no lunch for you," she said, and turned to Alex. "What are you doing? Don't waste your energy coming to the table to eat. Go to your room."

With a gasp, Alex began breathing, and walked back through the living room toward his bedroom. The phenomenon replayed over and over in his mind—the glass stopped falling, hanging in the air.

In the hallway, Sammy clutched Alex's arm and whispered with a voice full of amazement. "I can do magic."

Alex stopped, hand outstretched for his doorknob. *Can I...? Could it...?* "Yeah. Can't talk about it now."

Alex hurried into his room, snatched up the first thing he spotted, and threw it. As the videogame controller flew across the room, Alex reached out his hand and said, "Stop."

It crashed into the wall. Pieces of plastic flew everywhere. One piece hit and cut his hand. Alex stepped to the wall between his room and his cousin's. He knocked. In moments came an answering knock. Alex dropped to the floor by the air vent and whispered, "Sammy?"

"Yeah?"

"Try to make something stop falling by using your mind." Alex's heart pounded as he waited.

"Yes. I did it. It's amazing. Also, I can make it move."

The sound of his aunt's footsteps came from the hall. "Great. Got to go," Alex said. He hurried onto the bed, and the door opened.

"Here's some soup and a sandwich cut up small for you." Bending over, she set a tray down on the bed. Sunlight from the window illuminated the purple crystal she wore at her throat. "Take a nap after lunch."

Alex lay listening to noises coming from the rest of the house. Indistinctly he could make out Julia's voice in the distance. *How could Aunt Julia be so calm after the glass just hung in the air? She had to see it. Who's she talking to?*

Unable to contain his curiosity, he set his lunch on the floor and quietly went to his bedroom door. He heard only Julia's voice. *She's probably on the phone.*

"... you to watch the boys."

Is she going to leave? Alex lay back down breathing deeply, trying to calm himself. Sweat beaded on his forehead and stung as it rolled into his eyes. Just when he couldn't wait any longer, he heard her voice.

"Stay in your rooms. A babysitter will be here for a couple of days. I have to make a quick trip."

Slam! At the sound of the front door shuting, Alex jumped out of bed, ignored the sound of the soup splashing onto the floor, and hurried out of his room. His heart pounded loud and fast as he opened Sammy's door.

A sock weaved figure eights in the air. Alex snatched the sock out of the air and lay down on Sammy's bed. Looking up at Sammy, he said breathlessly, "I want you to heal me."

"What?" Sammy backed up with his mouth open.

"Put your hands on me and heal me," Alex said, desperation crackling in his voice.

"How?" Confusion on Sammy's face warred with the desire to help.

"I don't know." Alex sat up on the bed. He pleaded. "Try wanting it, just like you wanted the sock to move through the air."

Sammy stepped up closer to the bed. "Should I say something? Did the ministers who stopped at your hospital room try to heal you?"

"No." Alex reached out to Sammy with shaking hands. "Just try, please."

"Okay." Sammy stood still for a moment until he slowly reached his arms out putting his hands on Alex. "Be healed." And then much louder with more force, "Be healed."

After a long pause, Sammy asked, "Do you feel any different?"

Alex sat up, shaking from his emotions. "No."

Sammy fell into his older cousin's arms, both of them crying.

"Sammy, I don't want to die."

5

Chapter Three
The Aliens Arrive

A blaze of light blossomed in Earth's solar system. Out of the glare, a spaceship, the *Coratory*, burst forth. Inside its cavernous Hall of Flight, Ytell, an alien raptor with a thirty-foot wingspan, screeched. His piercing battle cry rent the air as his dark blue, almost black form, with a red breast, wheeled above a yellow and brown raptor.

Ytell's foe beat the air with his wings, trying to gain altitude, as he ranted to his supervisor. "This situation is stupid. We don't have enough time to save Earth."

"Our battle is supposed to be getting your mind off our problems." Ytell folded his wings, dropped into a steep dive, and tapped the other raptor's head with a fisted foot in passing. "You're hysterical. Focus on our fight, instead of the Earthlings' situation. I'd have a better fight with a fledgling. You're going to hurt yourself as distracted as you are."

The other raptor dove after Ytell, screaming his defiance.

The two raptors cartwheeled through the air. Wicked twelve-inch talons just missed Ytell dozens of times. In the aerial dance, Ytell slapped his sparring partner with a wing, and both of them fell two hundred feet toward the floor. Ytell beat his massive wings, rolled to the side, slipped past his foe, and slashed with one outstretched talon. A single, yellow feather fluttered away from the second raptor. Ytell beat his wings to back up and hover. "Well fought."

The second raptor flew away toward a balcony on the far wall of the Hall of Flight. "You were toying with me, but next time, I'll beat you." He grudgingly added, "Thanks for the fight. I do feel better."

Ytell wheeled about. A thousand feet away, a bipedal creature, Amable, stood watching from a balcony. *What does he want?* Stroking the air, Ytell studied his friend. Footlong tufts of lime-green and violet hair gently waved back and forth over Amable's ears, as he waited. Large, golden eyes circled with black in the pale face looked innocently back at Ytell. *He has his salesman smile on.* Snapping his beak together, Ytell beat his wings against the air. In a moment, he slammed down onto the balcony.

Amable said effusively, "Very impressive, Ytell. I've always said you raptors are amazing fighters. I'm glad to have you here."

Ytell turned his head to look with one of his yellowish-red eyes. The rising red ruff of feathers behind those eyes should've told Amable of the raptor's stirring anger. "We aren't just fighters. Do you forget why raptors are here? We have our dream of finding something greater than ourselves, even as we believe in and help your aspiration of saving worlds."

Amable held his hands out and slowly said, "Of course. We're all passionate about our dreams. I need to talk with you about the one-year trial."

Ytell snapped his beak. "A one-year trial isn't going to be enough time for the students of Earth. The—"

Amable smiled broadly. "You and I, we make the impossible—"

"Let me finish." Ytell lowered his hooked beak toward Amable's face. "The dominant species of Earth doesn't recognize any other species as being people. They have no communication or real understanding of the other people. The humans train some of the other species and have selectively bred some species to submit to their control. Humanity's focus on themselves as the only people will make it hard for humans and the other people of Earth to work together. It's not possible for the Earthlings to pass your one-year-test. After all the work we've done preparing to train Earthlings, it'd be a waste to not give them the full nine years of training."

Amable held both hands out and moved closer to his friend. "You're right. It would be a waste, but we've got a problem." Amable pointed up into the vast Hall of Flight at the Crystal of Jedh, a five-foot wide triclinic purple crystal hanging from the ceiling. For a moment both friends looked at its many jagged points. Amable quietly said, "We agree how horrible its creation was, but I'm not talking about that."

Ytell nodded his head.

At Ytell's nods, Amable shook his head. "My friend, I tell you, there's trouble. Trouble right here in the *Coratory*."

Ytell felt like shaking his head or thumping his friend's head. *I know what he's doing. He's selling me on something, and I'm getting sucked right into it.*

Amable said, "I'm telling you it's bad. So bad, I need you to give the Earthlings special focus in their training. And it's all because of the sabotage. Stick tells me due to the most recent damage, we'll be out of money in four years. It's a disaster."

"What do you want from me?" Ytell asked, ruffling his feathers back into place.

Amable waved his hands in a grand fashion. "Soon, we're going to find the new students on Earth. I need you and the other flock leaders to instruct them in working as a team to move large objects."

Why does Amable want this new training? It can't be done. Again the red ruff of feathers stood up around Ytell's head, and he lowered his beak until it almost touched Amable's face. As he spoke, his volume rose. "We don't have time. We already have too much to teach the Earthlings for them to pass your year-end test. They must get the other eight years of training."

Knocking Ytell's beak to the side, Amable glowered back at him. "And I say you have to add this to the training."

"Explain yourself."

The explanation didn't help, but after arguing back and forth, Ytell grumbled. "I don't like it, but I'll talk to the other flock leaders."

"Good," Amable said and turned to leave. Ytell watched him walk away. His ear tufts stood straight up on either side of his head like two horns of hair. *He isn't happy about this situation either.*

Lifting his head back between his folded wings, the seven-foot-tall Ytell stomped away. The annoyed scraping of his talons on the floor warned everyone an irritated raptor was coming. *Another decision to try to do the impossible, and who knows... maybe the universe or a god, if there is one, will take pity on us and again allow us to do the impossible.*

~**********~

Amable reached up to his throat, fingering a purple crystal. *Earthlings would call the gas within the crystal Dark Matter. His whole civilization relied on different forms of it. He needed the Dark Matter in the crystal, just like everyone on board the Coratory relied on the Dark Matter in the much bigger Crystal of Jedh. They used the crystal and its shards even though an abhorrent act of evil by deems created the crystal. Only two heroes leading a rebellion among the prisoners on this ship and then commandeering the Coratory from those deems enabled Amable and others to create the Academy and begin making real their dream of helping others survive against deems. That would make quite a story. Maybe I should have Stick look for a ghost writer. We could sell it.* Amable laughed at his ludicrous idea for getting money. *I'm ready to try anything, even if I know it's doomed to fail. Ytell's right. The Earthlings can't succeed. We'll barely keep the Academy running for the other students from planets we're already helping.*

Amable thought about the time when Dark Matter first comes to a world. The massive, sometimes terrible changes and deems come with Dark Matter. Amable's jaw clenched at the thought of deems. He had to get the Earthlings trained or Earth's life would be destroyed.

He marched down the corridors toward his office, where waiting outside was a thin, six-foot-tall bald creature, with gray fur.

"Sir, I have a report about the sabotage repairs."

Amable wasn't startled and didn't laugh at Stick's chartreuse, bulbous forehead, or the pencil-shaped, bright red nose that stuck straight out from his face. The universe had much stranger creatures and he became used to Stick and other peculiar people long ago. "Go ahead, Stick." Amable said, trying to be patient.

In a matter-of-fact tone Stick reported. "We will have to delay finding the students of Earth for two days until the repairs are done. Also, the investigation into the sabotage is inconclusive." His voice grew higher pitched and whiney. "The only good lead we have is a *kimley* boy found at the scene of the latest sabotage. He was stuck in an intra-ship portal. So far he has refused to cooperate with the investigation."

Amable interrupted. "Do we have any idea how he used the intra-ship portal?"

"No. That is one of the deem technologies we are still having trouble figuring out. Somehow, he or someone else knows how to use it. Because of past trouble, he has been confined to his quarters. Remember, I told you all of the young of the kimley species are trouble makers and need to be confined, or controlled in some manner." Stick paused to clear his throat. When he continued, it sounded as if someone had their hand around his neck threatening to rip off his colorful head. "There is one other thing."

"What is it? We don't have all day."

Stick reached up to rub his nose and as he did its color changed from bright red to variations of red, magenta, and purple. "I have received a report, but haven't been able to discern its veracity."

"And?"

Stick wiped some sweat off his bulging forehead. "Maleky is allegedly interested in Earth."

"Okay," Amable said calmly.

"Okay?" Stick asked, his voice rising to a squeak. "Is that all you have to say?"

"It's just a rumor for now." The door opened for Amable and he finished talking before entering his office. "Modify the security protocol of the computer to be on the lookout for creatures with dreadlocks. The stories about Maleky say he's allied with a species that sports dreadlocks."

Chapter Four
The Truth

Two days after Sammy tried to heal him, Alex lay in bed looking at the ceiling. His eyes burned from crying, and his guts felt twisted. He wished his parents were still alive. Mom and Dad believed in God and said they had faith in an eternity with God. He didn't know what he believed. He remembered one of the ministers not liking a game he played. She said there's magic that's evil, of the devil. God can do magical things, if there's a God. Is this his power?

Sammy barged into the bedroom. "Alex, I've got some kittens I saved from a dog."

Mewing came from a wriggling bulge in Sammy's shirt.

"Let me see," Alex said laughing. "The last time I petted some kittens, another boy accused me of being a sissy. When he realized a hot girl was playing with the kittens, he tried to pet the kittens too. She told him to get lost."

Soon the two cousins were petting and exclaiming over the kittens. A kitten squirmed into a pocket of Alex's cargo pants, causing him to laugh. Sammy had just replied that he had fed the kittens some milk already, when the boys heard a car pulling into the driveway.

"Quick, run the kittens out to the shed," Alex said.

Sammy stuffed the kittens into his shirt and ran for the backdoor. Alex eased out of bed and looked out his window. His aunt stood next to her car, gazing into the sky. Alex looked up, but the sky was empty.

She took the last bags out of the car as Alex heard the backdoor shut. In a moment, Sammy burst into Alex's room. "The kittens are safe."

"While you were outside, did you see anything in the sky?

12

"No," Sammy said. "Did something fly overhead?"

The front door slammed as Julia called, "Boys, come here."

Alex followed Sammy into the living room. His aunt held two necklaces with a silver pendant. "Put these on and leave them on."

"Why?" Sammy asked.

"Hush." She turned the TV on and started flipping through the channels. Finally, she paused on a news channel.

Alex gazed at his pendant before putting it on. It looked just like her purple pendant, and he looked up at her, wondering what was going on. The purple pendant at her neck was gone. In its place rested a silver pendant. He grabbed Sammy by the arm. "Come to my room."

Once they shut the door, Alex turned to Sammy. "Take off the necklace and try moving something."

Removing the necklace, Sammy gazed hard at a sock. The sock lay there. Alex grasped his little cousin's shoulder. "Something's wrong."

The voice of a newscaster came from the living room. "Now we go to a special broadcast from the White House. The next voice you hear will be the President's."

"Fellow Americans, people of Earth, we have made a great discovery, and like past discoveries it presents great opportunities for mankind.

"Mankind – the word has new meaning today. We can't hang onto old differences anymore. We are now united by the fact we are not alone."

Alex burst out of his room. In the living room, he saw his aunt standing behind the couch watching and listening to the TV. Alex asked, "What does he mean?" Meanwhile, the President continued speaking in the background.

"At this time we must reconsider the meaning of the word people, again because we are not alone. Let us not be timid. We face the unknown with courage, not because it is easy, but because it is hard."

Julia, her eyes riveted on the TV, said, "Other aliens have arrived."

Other aliens? The thought roared through Alex's mind. He was right. She wasn't one of the Blue Fugates. Why's she here? Is she really an alien? "What do you mean?" he demanded over the words of the President.

"This generation has been chosen to prove they are masters of themselves."

Now she turned away from the TV to smile at Alex. "Remember your suspicions about my blue skin? You were right."

Sammy huddled against Alex. "What's going on, Alex?"

Trying not to shake, Alex patted Sammy. "It's going to be all right."

The President's words continued, "… *Feast your eyes on those you love. Look at the beauties and splendors of Earth around you. You must reflect that your calm courage in the face of the unknown future is the only thing that will keep secure all you love."*

Julia looked down at Sammy. "Everything will be fine. I've been helping you focus on caring just for yourselves."

"What?" Alex asked. "Why are you doing this?"

"I was hired to prepare you for your future. You and Sammy both have important roles to play."

Looking confused and scared, Sammy said, "I want my daddy."

Alex backed away from her. *I've got to get Sammy out of here.* "Who's your boss?"

Julia picked up a small bag. A flickering, blue light shone forth from the bag, and she laughed as she spoke. "Sammy, you can't resist my influence in your life. Alex, my boss is in your head. He'll help you behave just the way he wants. You get irritated with my pushing Sammy to think only of himself. My boss doesn't care about anyone. He's in your mind right now, with his attitudes and with no feelings for others. You might think you're in control of who you are, but he's spiriting away who you were. It's actually for your own good. You won't be so weak after he's done."

Alex and Sammy gazed in horror at her. Around them, the President's words swirled.

14

"Remember the words of Winston Churchill, 'Danger: if you meet it promptly and without flinching, you will reduce the danger by half. Never run away from anything. Never!'"

Trying to sound more confident than he felt, Alex said, "I don't believe you. Your boss can't use us."

"I'm going to call Daddy," Sammy said.

Julia pulled a ball with flashing blue and white lights out of the bag.

Dread flooded through Alex. He desperately cried out, "Don't look at the ball, Sammy. Run to the door." Leaping across the room, Alex grasped the door handle.

"That's it, Sammy. Gaze at my ball."

"Sammy!" Alex yelled, releasing the handle. He looked back, and his eyes were captured by the flickering blue and white light.

Julia's voice filled his mind. "You will remember nothing of my strangeness, my being an alien, or the pendants. I am normal. Alex, after rescuing the kittens, you will not remember Sammy.

"Tomorrow after breakfast, you will go outside. Someone will be taking the little cats down to the pond. Alex, you will..."

As she continued placing instructions in Sammy and Alex's minds to prepare them for tomorrow's events, the President's cadenced voice spoke on.

"Robert Browning said, 'When the fight begins within himself, a man's worth something.' We do not know the future, but we must face it with hope and faith in a good future. We must fight first to be what we would be."

The words of the President and Julia merged in Alex's mind, and then all was quiet. He blinked. With a yawn, Alex said, "I'm tired. Goodnight."

Sammy said, "I'm tired. Goodnight."

~**********~

On the *Coratory*, Amable stood in his office watching a creature called a fish-plant with its large, liquid-filled leaves dancing to its own song, the *Ode of Remembrance*. Amable blinked back tears, as the vibrations from the low notes flowed through his body. Within the leaves, small blue and silver creatures swam back and forth to the beat.

The gentle movements of the fish-plant tugged at Amable's heart, until he knelt on his knees in front of them. They were the last creatures alive from their world. He ground the heels of his hands into his forehead. *I'm sorry we got there too late. I feel your pain and anger. We will defeat the deem.*

Hesitantly, Amable reached up to his ears and removed a film protecting his emotions from the words of the *song*. A phrase set to the deep, melancholy ringing of bells repeated again and again.

Our water's gone, our lives just drifting motes of dust.

Other voices at the same time sung verses set to a higher octave, but still low and unbearably sad.

They tore my friends and family to eternal night.
No fergins fly, only those creatures of blight.

A tear ran down Amable's cheek, as the words of the people long dead tore at his heart. A pounding noise made him look down. His fist pounded against the floor.

Looking at the wall behind the plant, Amable gave a command to the computer via his Artificial Intelligence (AI), |Show me Earth from here.| The plain white wall disappeared replaced by the view of Earth from their low orbit.

A knock at Amable's door interrupted his thoughts. The view of Earth disappeared as Amable said, "Open."

The door opened, and Stick stepped toward Amable, falling on his bony knees as the music of remembrance hit him. Between sobs, he gasped. "Pain..., the pain... of the loss... is too much."

Moving quickly, Amable swept up the filmy ear blockers off his desk and thrust them against Stick's ears.

Stick continued to sob for a while, taking great gulping breaths of air. He struggled to his feet. "Sorry, sir. The sorrow in that song brings back the pain of losing my own world. Thank you for the blockers."

Shuddering, Stick took a deep breath, his jaw muscles clenched, his mouth mashed into its normal straight line. "Repairs are done. Do you want to be at the control station before we release the Dark Matter into Earth's atmosphere? Also, I need your signature on this paperwork."

A three-dimensional hologram of paperwork appeared in front of him.

Amable answered via his AI communication because Stick couldn't hear with the blockers on. |Don't wait for me. When we're finally ready, I'm going directly to the shuttle. I'll be leaving with my team to collect the students.|

Stick nodded, as he heard the message in his head and said, "What about the paperwork?"

Amable sighed to himself and answered. |Ah paperwork, can't forget that. You'd think saving planets would take less paperwork.|

"No, sir, of course not. Paperwork is far too important. Sign right here." Stick maneuvered the holographic paperwork, and Amable reached into the holographs to touch his finger to the right places. "Sign here. One more here. Oh— and another here. Thank you, sir."

|Is that all, Stick?|

"For now, sir. Oh sorry, sir, I almost forgot these." Another set of holographic forms appeared in the air.

Amable backed away. |And what are these?|

"Permission to create more paperwork."

"To create *more* paperwork," repeated Amable to himself.

"We need paperwork for each of the new students. The exculpatory agreements are the most important part of the process."

|I suppose, I'll have to take releases and waivers of liability to Earth for parents and students to sign.| Amable told Stick with a rueful shake of his head. Now, he was recruited to foist the evil of paperwork onto others. Another thought froze Amable. *This is a disaster.* |Stick, we have a problem. Because of the delays caused by the sabotage, we aren't recruiting the students. Instead, we're *abducting* them. No one will sign the students' paperwork.|

"Already taken care of, sir. Just finish your signatures. I've spoken to the PETA representative about it, and she agrees that Earthlings are subcategory creatures. She'll sign for all of them."

After the last signature, Stick stepped to the doorway. "I told you we needed to work with the People for Ethical Treatment of Aliens."

The door shut behind Stick, and the Ode of Remembrance played on in counterpoint to Amable's thoughts, as he clenched his fists. Paperwork really wasn't evil. What the deems would do to Earth was evil. I must save this planet.

We are lost, the screams of the dying are fading.

Sorrow eats joy, night creatures fear for hope trading.

With the distraction of Stick gone, Amable sank into a sea of emotions. Sweat broke out on Amable's forehead, and his teeth began to ache from being clenched. They had saved members from many of Earth's religions from the coming disaster. The representatives of those religions had been helping them understand the ways of life on Earth. This time those deems were going to lose. If only he could believe it.

Our culture whispers in the wind, do you hear?

The wicked go unpunished, they laugh with no fear.

Amable growled, "Open my closet." A section of wall opposite the plant dissolved away, revealing a new three-foot wide, bat-like model hanging in a small room. Its small eyes glowed red. Fangs glistened in the partially open maw.

Around him, the melancholy music continued, as with a grunt, Amable lifted an ornate metal bar from the floor. He swung the heavy bar and hit the model. "We're going to win!" He smashed the model again and again. Between ragged breaths for air, he declared, "Your kind won't destroy all the life of this world. I'm taking students from Earth. In one year, I'll know if Earth's species can work together to save Earth. If they can't work together, I'll save what I can before your kind get here and destroy Earth's life."

His team was going to inject Dark Matter into Earth's atmosphere, and a few of Earth's creatures would respond by doing unexplainable things. Once Amable took those affected from Earth, he'd transform them into tools for life.

Never more will winter prime and winter second change life.

Strangeness fell on us, the night creatures devoured our life.

Dust from the destroyed model settled around Amable. With a clang, he dropped the bar to the floor. *For Earth's sake, I hope these students can learn to work together.* Brushing the dust and chips off his clothes, he left the closet and then his office. He heard the descant again just before his door shut. In his closet a new creation hung waiting for the next therapy session.

Our water is gone, our lives just motes of dust drifting.

Chapter Five
Abducting Students

That night, Alex had a nightmare. A green snake with dreadlocks slithered up to Sammy and wrapped scaly coil after coil around him and started squeezing.

The snake wore his aunt's face, and it leered at Alex. "I'm modifying Sammy's personality. He's going to be just like me."

Shouting, "Never!" Alex grappled with the snake, trying to save Sammy, but the snake inflated, floated up into the air, and lifted Alex higher and higher. Below him, Sammy waved goodbye.

Alex's eyes popped open, and the dream slipped from his mind. A green pendant rested on his nightstand and without thinking, he removed the silver one and put on the new one.

Heading to the kitchen he passed his aunt, as she went toward her room muttering. "Where did the milk and the cream go?"

In the kitchen, Sammy was rummaging in the refrigerator. "I need to feed the kittens, but we're out of milk, and I already used the whipping cream."

In jest, Alex suggested, "Maybe they could eat ice cream."

Sammy grabbed the ice cream from the freezer and scooped some out into a bowl. Just after Sammy jammed the ice cream back into the freezer, Alex heard Julia coming. He whispered, "Dump the ice cream in the garbage."

Sammy whispered back, "No, the kittens need it."

The sounds of steps grew louder as Alex whispered, "Hide it."

Sammy scooped the ice cream out of the bowl, jammed it into one of Alex's cargo pockets, and put the bowl in the dishwasher.

Shock and the desire to be quiet warred in Alex. One word exploded out of him. "Hey."

"Sammy, what are you up to?" Julia asked as she came into the room.

"Uh, going outside with Alex."

Cold on his leg made Alex want to squirm.

"Why is the dishwasher open? I've told you not to load the dishwasher."

Dampness seeped through Alex's pants. He grabbed Sammy's hand. "The dishwasher was open when we came in here. I was just going to shut it. We're going for a walk."

Julia crossed the kitchen, hugged Alex, and gave him a quick kiss on the forehead. "Good. Goodbye and good luck. I'm going to miss you." She handed him a vial. "Drink this. You'll need the extra energy."

With these words, Sammy opened the door saying, "Come on, Alex!"

Ignoring the strangeness of her giving him a vial of liquid to drink, Alex paused to drink it, and followed Sammy out into the yard. Frost coated the grass. A shed stood among tall trees on the other side of the yard. From the building, a path trailed downhill toward a distant pond. The shed door swung gently in the breeze. Alex grasped his pants and started turning the pocket inside out. Laughing at the cold sensation of melting ice cream, he said, "Sammy, take the ice cream out of my pocket."

The sound of kittens crying in alarm interrupted their conversation, and in response, they ran. The figure of a stranger with black dreadlocks emerged from the dark interior of the shed. From the burlap bag he carried came piteous meows.

Sammy yelled, "Don't hurt them!"

The man loped down the trail. Alex sprinted after him. Stumbling, running, and panting, he followed down the hill. His initial burst of energy faded. A root snagged his foot. With a lurch, he tumbled down to the pond stopping only at the edge of the ice.

Sammy crashed to a stop, as Alex struggled back to his feet. The last leaf from a nearby tree drifted past in the cold, gentle breeze. Their breath formed small clouds of fog. The faint cries of kittens came from the sack out on the frozen pond.

Sammy asked, "What are we going to do?"

Still panting from the chase, Alex put one foot onto the ice. "We... have to... help them." Carefully, he put weight on the ice. The ice cracked with barely any of his weight. A frown crossed his face at a transient thought. It was like Alex had no choice, and the events of him rescuing the kittens had all been planned out. Time and the rescue of the kittens passed like the fog of his breath.

"What are we going to do with the kittens?" Sammy asked, as he stuffed them into his shirt.

"Take them to our neighbor, Mr. Hall."

Alex leaned more and more on Sammy, as they walked up the hill. Almost at the top of the hill Alex stopped. A thought, not his own, pounded inside his head. *You must go on alone.*

Alex looked down at Sammy. He started to say something, but emotions not connected to his thoughts choked his throat and one word came out. "Bye."

With one hand, he removed the crystal pendant and dropped it. Julia would retrieve the expensive device later. It had done its job for her, and now Alex followed the last of Julia's hypnotic instructions.

The dreadlock man stepped between Alex and Sammy. Alex turned away forgetting both Sammy and the dreadlock man.

From behind him came a child's pleading voice, "Let go of me."

"Sammy, you can't go with him," A man said.

The child cried out, "Alex, help!"

Confusion filled Alex's mind. Who were those people back there? The hypnosis overrode the question, and he continued up the hill. The sound of a TV came from a neighbor's house. The rumble of a truck's engine pulled his attention to the street, and then the noise of the TV and the engine died. He saw the truck coast to a stop.

A chill rippled down his back as a heavy fog swallowed everything up. Shadows moved in the fog, and Alex backed up.

22

Thick, tough-looking hands reached out from the fog to grasp him. He tried to get away, but the day's activities and his illness had caught up to him. Alex collapsed. He felt something being done behind his ear, and someone else fastened something around one of his ankles. The cold of the ground seeped into his bones. Everything around him faded away.

The sound of sirens drew Alex back to consciousness. He opened his eyes to fog. Frantic, he tried to get up, but he couldn't move his body. A scream burst from him. "Aah! Help!" The sirens came closer.

A man called out, "Who's out there!"

"Over here! Help me!"

"Keep shouting," the man said. "This strange fog is making it hard to find you."

The ground fell away from under him. Misty tendrils of fog streamed past. Sunshine struck his face. Blinded by the light, scared, and confused, one thought screamed in his mind. *I'm being abducted.* Something above him drew nearer, and then it blocked the sun. Alex was pulled up into the object and through a tube. Lights flashed quickly by, until he popped from the tube.

A cacophony of sounds assaulted him, as his body settled onto a large, yellow disc. A sharp pungent smell, like ozone, assailed his nose, and he sneezed. After rolling over, Alex struggled to his knees. A shimmering wall of yellow light rose from the edge of his disc. Placing his hand on the wall of light he felt it give a little, before hardening. Other discs of different colors with their own walls, prisons of light, floated around him. Each prison held a person or animal. Above the disc nearest Alex, a dolphin somehow floated and moved in the air, and they stared at each other. *What does it think of being captured, and given the ability to move in the air, like it's water?*

A quiet voice called to Alex. "Are you okay?"

Looking around he saw a girl positioned on her back, covered by a blanket, surrounded by a blue haze, and floating in the air above a yellow prison disc with a yellow wall of light. Around the base of her head the haze was pink and tiny bright

23

lights orbited in the haze. The back of her head was shaved and angry, red puckered skin gave evidence of a wound or surgery. Three braids hung from the side of her head. One of those braids started at the center of her forehead. Small reddish gold ringlets stuck to her face, big blue eyes stared right at him.

"Yes, I'm talking to you," she said, in heavily accented words.

"What's going on? Where are we?" Alex asked.

"I don't know where we are, but I'm free. It's great. I'm A'idah. What about you? You're all hunched over and pale. Are you okay?"

Alex stood up straight, trying to keep his balance. "I'm fine. I'm Alex. How can you be so calm? We've been... we've been..."

"Abducted?" A'idah asked. "Yes. We have been and they appear to be sorting us. Me? Calm? Ha. That's funny. I'm so excited. I haven't been able to talk for six months. At first my voice was all croaky and it hurt to talk. A boy brought me a drink. It's helped. The aliens understand us. I complained about how indecent this hospital garment is, and they brought me a blanket. About the abduction thing, these aliens better be careful. I won't put up with— Oh, look one of the boys is bringing you a drink."

Looking around Alex noticed prison discs sliding across the floor, and the same colored discs were moving together. A white-haired boy with fine features and pointy ears sticking out of his hair stood staring at him with large eyes. He wore a simple white shirt with billowing sleeves. Over the shirt a tight green and orange vest hugged his torso. Very faintly, tentatively, a song started to play in Alex's mind and stopped. A flush darkened the boy's face and he looked down.

Another white-haired boy carrying a glass walked past a snow leopard just as the snow leopard's disc changed to a dark-blue. The leopard stood on its disc, ears flat against its skull, and tail lashing. A rustling sound above drew Alex's attention. On perches, shadowy forms with huge wings jostled each other. In his fear and confusion, Alex didn't notice his fatigue or his struggle to breathe.

Then a voice spoke strange words near him. One of the white-haired boys stood by Alex just outside the wall of light. The boy's temples had a strange color. *He looks like an elf.* He held a tall glass with some liquid. Alex gasped as the boy pushed the glass through the wall of light. Quickly Alex tried to push his hand through the wall, but it bounced back. The boy laughed and pointed to the glass.

"He wants you to take the drink," A'idah said. "Go ahead. It's okay, I had some earlier."

"Can you understand him?" Alex asked.

"I... I can and the dolphin over there. He misses his family. The big blue bird wants some nuts. Oh my, it's so crazy," A'idah said her voice shaking. She moved her hand and tears started to trickle down her cheek. "Alex, look, I can move my hand."

The wall of light surrounding Alex changed to a dark-blue and his disc started carrying him away.

"Alex, don't go," A'idah pleaded. "Come back."

Alex shoved hard against the wall of light. He just bounced back. A small hand tugged on his sleeve. It was the strange white-haired boy. The boy grasped Alex's hand and pulled it toward the wall. Alex's hand and arm went through the wall of light. Pain lanced through him as he passed through the prison, but he gritted his teeth and held on to the small hand. The suffering passed as Alex stepped off his disc. The shouts of humans and cries of animals increased. Loud piercing whistles filled the air. The boy tugged on Alex's hand. Alex tried to go faster, but his feet dragged. Reaching A'idah's disc the boy shoved Alex through the yellow wall of light. Stumbling, Alex took A'idah's hand. "Don't cry, we'll be alright."

"Look out! Behind you!" A'idah yelled.

Amongst all of the strange smells came a blast of cinnamon. Alex twisted around as a gust of wind struck him. The yellow wall of light vanished. A seven-foot tall bird with a bright red crest around its head landed. From under its wings two thin arms reached out for him. Alex batted them aside.

"Alex," A'idah said. "He says you need to go to your disc."

"I'm not leaving you," Alex said.

The bird's hooked beak darted down and roughly grasped Alex's shoulder. He could feel the point of the cruel beak tearing through his shirt. He swung a fist at the bird's head and felt it connect with an eye. The beak released Alex. Massive wings beat the air. A'idah screamed. Alex backed up, fists up, weaving, and fighting dizziness. The wings stopped beating. A green and white striped cow came running up. Alex crumbled and everything went dark.

Chapter Six
A'idah gets to know Alex

A'idah walked through the corridors of the alien spaceship. She wore loose cream colored pants and shirt. Over her head was a black scarf with red, yellow, and orange embroidery. Beside her, a dolphin swam through the air. The changes in the last days almost overwhelmed her. Five days ago, she lay in a hospital suffering from what the doctors called *locked in.* She had been totally paralyzed by a gunshot without any hope of recovery. Her hospital stay was horrible. At first, she missed her group of friends. Loneliness and fear closed in on her, but as a month went by anger replaced those feelings.

Miraculously, one day she began to recover. First feelings on her face and the ability to blink came back. The aliens arrived minutes after the miracle began. One of them poured a blue liquid over her. It turned into a blue haze and she felt herself lift off the bed and float in the air. The aliens worked quickly, disconnected her from the equipment, took her down the hall, and out of the hospital. It was scary, but she felt herself continuing to improve. She'd focused on her miraculous recovery; she refused to let the abduction frighten her. She was going to be free to move and do what she wanted. It amazed her to see all of the people standing still in the hospital as she floated past.

On the spaceship, she floated above a disc, and all of those other humans and animals on discs were held captive by shimmering walls of light. Then, Alex arrived onto a disc near her. He was like her, a fighter. No one was going to stop him. Alex found a way off his disc to come to her aid. She could tell he liked her. *It's too bad he isn't a girl.* She didn't know how to deal with a boy for a friend. The seven-foot tall alien raptor, later she found out he was Ytell, made the mistake of attacking Alex. Alex showed him. He hit Ytell hard in his eye. Alex was wonderful. She felt so proud watching him fight. She wanted to fight beside him. All she could do was spit at Ytell. When Alex fell to the floor she screamed. "What have you done to him? I'm going to kill you!" Zeghes, the dolphin, beat himself against his barrier of light trying to aid her and Alex, until he collapsed. Alex and Zeghes were her new group of friends. Zeghes called them his pod or family.

It was a good thing for the aliens she finally started to understand what they were saying. She had struggled to stand. She wasn't going to let them hurt Alex. A cow-like creature told Ytell to leave the human alone. A different alien with four arms and green bushy hair ran to him pushing Ytell out of the way. She poured a liquid over Alex, and it turned into blue haze, except for around his head. Around his head, it was pink. The aliens were surprised to find out A'idah could understand them. Her mind learned faster than they expected to work with that thingy they put behind her ear.

Those aliens thought they could abduct earthlings, because they were in a hurry, instead of explaining first to let earthlings choose. That was garbage. You don't treat people that way. A'idah couldn't stay mad. She kept grinning whenever she thought about getting to talk to the snow leopard and the big blue bird. Zeghes, the dolphin, was particularly great. She loved him. But she'd been worried about Alex. The pink haze meant he had some kind of illness in his head. She visited him every day. Her new friend, Zeghes, believed sick people shouldn't be left alone. Gursha, the green haireded nurse, said he was supposed to regain consciousness today.

A'idah paused at the final corridor before the clinic. *What if Alex doesn't like me? What if he doesn't respect me?* She desperately needed his friendship. Briefly she considered her girlfriends back in the Hindu Kush Mountains. How she missed them. If only Alex was a girl. What if he's not the hero she thought him to be? What if he thinks all women without family are just asking to be mistreated, or that a woman is only worth half of a man? She cracked her knuckles. *He'll get hurt and I've got Zeghes for family. I will be free.* A'idah shouted at Zeghes, "Wait up. I have to be the first to see him."

Zeghes twisted back in the air to face her. "Stop trying to tell me what to do. Girls aren't supposed to order guys about."

A'idah ducked past him to enter the nurse's clinic. "Get used to it Zeghes. I'm not a dolphin."

Gursha, the matronly four-armed nurse greeted them. "You're just in time." She turned to Alex. "Alex, wake-up. Some of your flock members are here to meet you."

Alex lay surrounded by a blue haze, except for a pink haze around his head. He floated about three feet off the ground. Alex blinked and turned his head toward them.

"Hi, Alex," Zeghes said. "Don't worry about any danger. Zeghes is here. That's me. The girl is A'idah. You go ahead and talk to her. I'm going to patrol the area for sharks."

"Uh, hi," Alex said weakly. "There was another dream before this." He paused. "I slugged a giant bird."

"Hi," A'idah said and turned to Gursha. "Are you sure he's ready for company?"

"He's just a bit groggy. He needs to get up for a while," the nurse said.

"I like this dream. It's better than the first one."

"It isn't a dream," A'idah said.

"I like having you in this dream. You're cute."

"Gursha!" A'idah exclaimed, feeling a warmth travel up her neck.

Gursha hummed to herself. "He must be suffering side effects of his treatment. I'll make a change to his holo field. He should be better in a second."

Alex struggled to sit up. "Where am I? What's going on? Why is everything pinkish? You're the girl I saw in my dream."

"Whoa, one question at a time," A'idah said. "You sound just like Zeghes. When he first talked to me, he had so many questions. Don't you remember meeting me?"

"No, who are you?"

Doesn't he remember fighting for me? "I'm the girl you just called cute. We met on the shuttle."

Alex's face turned red. "I'm sorry."

A'idah put her hands on her hips. "You mean I'm not cute?"

"Uh, no, I mean…" Alex said turning redder. "Where am I?"

"You're on a spaceship with other people and animals from Earth. We were on discs and you got in a fight with Ytell because of me. Ytell wants me to apologize for him. My name's A'idah," she said with a grin. "I think you were great."

"It really happened?" Alex asked. "You're free. What happened?" Alex stared past A'idah at Gursha. "You've got four arms!"

"It's an alien spaceship and they're helping us," A'idah said. "She's our nurse, Gursha."

"Wow." Alex looked down and with alarm bordering on hysteria said, "What's holding me up?"

"It's a medical holo field," Gursha said. "It serves as a bed and provides diagnostics and treatment."

Alex took a deep breath.

"How're you feeling?" A'idah asked, in a concerned tone.

Standing up, struggling with a flood of emotions, and stretching, Alex said, "I feel good. What's happened to me? And the pinkish haze is gone."

"The medical holo field turned itself off after you stood up," said Gursha.

A'idah said, "We're both getting healed because of something called Dark Matter."

"What? Healed? You mean I'm not going to die?" Alex gazed at her in shock, and then ran around the room until he stopped, bending over, panting.

"Wow," he said, after catching his breath. "I'm so much better. How? Why?"

"We're here because we react to a substance called Dark Matter. In about nine years Earth's solar system will move into an area of the galaxy where there's lots of it. Other life on Earth will respond to Dark Matter, and deems will attack Earth. We're going to be trained so we can save Earth."

Alex smiled at A'idah. "I'm not dying anymore. You said you're being healed. What happened to you?"

"I was totally paralyzed."

"What happened? You can walk now."

"This was my experience. I was lying in bed and.... As she spoke she remembered the events. It was as if they were happening for the first time.

I need to shut my eyes. Oh why can't I at least shut my eyes? That nurse left the patches off my eyes on purpose when she left. I know she brought this fly in. The fly is at my eye. It's going to step on my eye and I can't close it. Why did the doctor tell me I'm totally paralyzed. He has to be wrong. I need to shut my eyelid. It's on my eye, oh gross, oh no, help me. Shut eye, shut eye, work nerves. The doctor's wrong. My eyelids shut, oh glory.

There are tears on my face. I can feel them. This is wonderful. This is, oh, I can feel and move. Someone come and see. Please, someone come and see me. Let me show you what I can do and feel. Someone come and take these tubes out of my throat. I can breathe on my own. This is great. Oh wow. Oh my. I'm going to be normal.

"That was the beginning of a wonderful change for me. Because of my reaction to Dark Matter, I started to heal myself. These aliens put Dark Matter into Earth's atmosphere to find creatures that react to Dark Matter. Healing is what I did on Earth. What about you? What did you do?" A'idah asked Alex.

Momentarily Alex looked confused. "I rescued some kittens. They were in a burlap bag in the middle of a pond. I had to crawl across really thin ice. The ice cracked, and water started to flow across the ice, but then the water froze instantly, and on my way back to shore the ice started to break again. I thought I was going to get a cold dip in the pond. Somehow I became so light a gentle breeze blew me up above the pond and into some willows."

"You froze the water and made yourself lighter?"

"I guess so."

Zeghes swam back into the room. "All safe. No sharks,"

"A dolphin, right here, in the air-he's swimming in the air and talking to me," Alex said in amazement.

"He's been given some kind of fancy suit," A'idah said nonchalantly, as she smiled at Alex. "It makes him able to swim through the air, just like he's still in the water."

"How can he talk?"

"Dolphins have always talked. It's because of squirts that we finally understand."

"What're squirts?"

"Small organisms placed behind our ears. They're why we can understand the animals."

Alex's hand started to move up to his ear. "This is crazy. Are there sharks up here?"

"On Earth we always watched for sharks," Zeghes said. "I'm told there are no sharks here. But I still watch."

"Can I touch you?" Alex asked Zeghes.

"Sure thing."

"I can feel the suit you're wearing, and yet it lets my hand through to touch your skin. This is amazing. I'm going to live and..." Tears cascaded down his face. Zeghes rubbed against him.

Giving in to his need for comfort, A'idah hugged Alex. "Hey, I understand. I bawled like a baby forever after I began to move and feel again." Holding Alex made her think of her grandmother's words. *Don't be frightened by the changes that will come. Remember how I've taught you to behave as a woman. Don't be stupid and let any man talk you into sleeping together. Your father's right about keeping your distance from boys that aren't family. But don't let him take your freedom as a Kalasha woman. The Muslims have filled his mind with their doctrine. At least good Muslims would treat you right.* Her grandmother and father's disagreements still tore at her heart. She liked what her grandmother said, but hated hurting her father.

Grandmother's adamant words continued in her mind. *In our culture the women are free. It's good for Kalasha women to be seen. We get to choose our mates. If we don't like our husbands, we can leave them at any time. Remember when you're a woman and hug a man it's good for him to be a bit shy, but you want him to enjoy it. The ones who are too shy make good friends, but don't consider them as a mate. Look for someone who has things in common with you. Don't wait too long to choose your man. Also, be careful, A'idah. There'll be those who'll take advantage of a hug and expect more. Some around us expect they can take advantage of us, because we're different.* A'idah thought, it's embarrassing to hug a boy. She felt Alex relaxing his hold on her. Letting go of Alex, she stepped back. *Oh, he's blushing. Good or is he blushing too much? This is so confusing. I just want a friend. Why couldn't he be a girl?*

"Thanks for holding me," Alex said. "Sorry I lost it."

Two white haired boys wearing colorful outfits ran out of the room. *Uh, oh. It's the kimley boys.* A'idah looked down at her feet and then at Alex's feet. "Wait!"

She spoke too late. Alex started to take a step. "When did those—?" He tipped forward, thin arms windmilling, and grabbed for A'idah. Missing, he fell down. "Ah!"

Laughing, A'idah said, "Sorry for laughing about your shoes being tied together. The Soaley boys seem to victimize everyone. They're kimleys, one of the many different kinds of aliens you're going to meet."

The sound of heavy footsteps came from the doorway and the smell of cinnamon filled the air. A'idah looked up from Alex to see a dark blue, almost black raptor entering the clinic. It was Ytell. Quickly she stepped in-between Alex and Ytell and craned her neck to look up at Ytell's face. "You came too soon."

"Lookout A'idah," Alex said, scrambling to his feet. "It's the alien who bit me."

Ytell tipped his head to consider A'idah with one yellowish-red eye. "I'm sorry. Haven't you explained to Alex what's going on?"

Zeghes dove at Ytell and rammed into him. "You need to leave Alex alone. He's still sick. You can't catch us and shove us around like you do. It isn't right."

Ytell backed up, as Alex and A'idah both spoke at the same time.

A'idah poked at Ytell's dark-red breast with her finger. "Zeghes is right. You need to leave Alex alone. We're informing him about what's going on."

Alex hopped forward. "Don't hurt my friend." he said falling against A'idah, taking both of them down onto Ytell's scaly, blue feet.

Gursha bustled forward, and Zeghes drifted out of her way. Her voice resonated with authority and irritation. "You Earthlings be quiet and wait. Ytell, you're hurt. Come over here."

Shaking his head, Ytell pulled his feet out from under the two humans. "I can..."

Gursha interrupted him with a glare and pointed to a pattern on the floor. After taking a step Ytell paused, and shuffled the rest of the way to the pattern.

A blue haze rose up lifting Ytell. It turned pink around the area Zeghes had hit. Gursha muttered to herself, one set of hands on her hips and with the other set reached into the haze. "You didn't have to let him break your ribs."

Ytell said, "Zeghes could've gotten hurt, and fighting with him would slow down his acclimatization. We've already caused him trouble adjusting. He thinks I'm the equivalent of a shark. For Earth's sake, all of the Earthlings must progress quickly."

Gursha pulled her hands out of the haze as some of the pink turned to blue. "Okay, your ribs have begun to knit. I don't suppose you'll stay until they're completely mended?"

"No."

The blue haze faded away, lowering Ytell to the ground. He stretched and slightly opened his wings. Shaking his feathers, he closed his wings back against his body. Gursha frowned and stepped closer to him. "Don't fly during the next few days and come back if it starts hurting again."

"Thank you," Ytell said.

Gursha said. "Of course, you won't come back because of a little pain. Since you're too stubborn to stay until you're healed, you need to leave. This has been too much excitement for my other patient."

Ytell turned to Alex. "I'm Ytell, your flock leader. I'll see you tomorrow morning." Then he left with a swish of his feathers.

A'idah laughed a short nervous laugh and said, "We showed him."

A grin replaced the scowl on Alex's face, as he joined A'idah in laughter. "I guess we did."

Gursha came over, helped Alex and A'idah back on their feet. When Alex stood on his feet again, he said, "Thanks, Gursha." With a confused look he added, "How come my shoes are no longer tied together?"

Gursha continued to hold A'idah by the arm, and spoke to Alex. "The Soaley boys use something that evaporates after a little while. Do you see that pattern on the floor?"

"Yes."

"Go sit down in the air over it. The holo field will respond to your thoughts and support you."

"Okay." Alex turned around and awkwardly sat in midair. A blue haze appeared around his body, supporting him in a sitting position. "What did Ytell mean about causing Zeghes trouble?"

A'idah tried to pull away from Gursha and said, "After Zeghes was torn from his pod in the abduction, he saw you fight Ytell, one of the abductors. That caused him to bond with you and me as his new pod. Which means we're his new family. However, it also caused his aggression towards Ytell. He has Ytell confused with his idea of sharks. The PETA rep says Ytell has to allow it, per a signed agreement. She says Zeghes will eventually heal from the abduction trauma, and the aggression toward Ytell will stop."

For a long second Alex just stared at A'idah. His mouth opened and shut. Finally, he said, "So now you, Zeghes, and I are family? I like that idea. I'll try and be a good big brother for him and you."

Gursha shook A'idah by the arm she held. "A'idah?"

"What?" A'idah tried again to pull away. *It was fun getting Alex to defend me again.*

"Young lady," Gursha said, glowering at A'idah. "You forgot your responsibility to Alex. We talked about this during your visits here."

35

Alex looked back and forth between the two of them. A'idah opened her mouth to reply, but Gursha held up a hand, keeping two firmly on her hips.

"Don't excuse yourself to me," Gursha said. "Tell Alex what he needs to know."

A'idah looked at Alex and then down at his feet. *What's Alex going to think?* "I'm sorry. I should've talked about this sooner before Ytell arrived. I told him I would."

"What?" Alex asked.

"Get on with it," Gursha said.

A'idah looked up into Alex's eyes. "I knew that Ytell was just coming to talk to you, and he has checked up on you every day. He's been concerned about your health. Also, he wasn't attacking you on the day of your abduction and won't attack you. They needed to finish sorting out the flocks, and Alex, you were holding things up. They couldn't leave Earth until they finished. Ytell is worried about having enough time to help us. We must accomplish something before the year is up, or the aliens will give up on Earth. Which would mean everyone on Earth dies."

A'idah paused, breathing deep, and her eyes glistened. Gursha pulled her close. "If you had said that sooner, Alex wouldn't have reacted to Ytell the way he did, which might've kept Zeghes from attacking Ytell."

"I'm sorry.... For not telling him sooner," A'idah said.

"That's enough visiting for now. I want all of you out," Gursha said.

"I should stay with Alex," Zeghes said stubbornly. "Sick pod members should not be left alone."

"He'll be fine, Zeghes," Gursha said.

A'idah paused at the door not wanting to leave. "Thanks for standing up to Ytell for me, Alex."

Alex said, "Family have to stand up for each other and don't worry about not having told me all that stuff before Ytell arrived. When I saw him again I still would've reacted the same way."

Stopping just outside the clinic A'idah considered what had happened. Was hugging him the right thing to do? She knew both of them needed the hug. She wished her

36

grandmother could be with her. *I think I've found a friend my grandmother would approve of, and he's kinda family now. He would defend me from the terrorists back on Earth.* Firmly A'idah smothered the memories of her girlfriend's pain. She heard Gursha speaking to Alex.

"Now I want you to eat some of the food on that cart," Gursha said. "I'll be right next door. Let me know when you're done eating."

"Thanks for helping me." Alex said. "What's this band on my ankle?"

"You're welcome. I enjoy taking care of others," Gursha said. A moment of silence followed and A'idah heard Gursha's voice. "That's a temporary thing, a civilization bracelet. Soon it will be...."

Zeghes bumped A'idah from behind. "What are you doing?"

A'idah looked at Zeghes for a moment before saying, "I don't want to leave, but I guess we'll see him tomorrow."

Chapter Seven
Alex Gets Surprised

The next day, after a tasty breakfast Gursha took him to join his flock. As Alex walked his heart beat faster. *I get to see Zeghes and A'idah again. What will the rest of the group be like? I think I can hear Zeghes.* The door slid open, but Gursha blocked his view.

"Now, I'm leaving you with your flock. As I told you on the way here, I know of no finer flock leader than Ytell. You just had a bad start with him. Now let me hug you. Just because you're a teenager doesn't mean Gursha can't hug you."

It's strange getting hugged by four arms.

Releasing her hold, Gursha ruffled his hair. "You have a good day. I'll see you this evening."

A sudden wave of loss rolled over Alex. *That's what Mom used to do before she died.* A tear rolled down his cheek and he quickly wiped it away.

A'idah stepped through the doorway and took his hand. "Are you okay?"

"I'm fine," Alex said, struggling to control his emotions and followed A'idah through the doorway into chaos. In front of Alex, Zeghes swam through the air swatting Ytell with his tail. "Whoops Ytell, I don't have this suit all figured out yet."

A snow leopard played with a big, blue bird's tail.

The bird yelled, "You do that again and I'll bite your tail off."

A man with gray hair pointed at a ledge. "Sabu, jump up on that ledge and stay there."

The snow leopard leapt on the man's back, and knocked him down as she jumped onto the ledge. She lay down, her long tail twitching.

38

Alex's mouth dropped open as he looked around the room. He'd never seen such an interesting group interacting all at once.

Ytell, at seven feet tall with his piercing eyes and dangerous-looking hooked beak, commanded attention as he opened his beak to talk. "Good morning, Alex. Let me introduce the rest of your flock. Sabu is the snow leopard on the ledge."

As her thick tail twitched, Sabu said, "I don't want to be part of this."

"Why don't you?" Alex asked.

Sabu pulled her lips back to show her teeth and looked at the gray-haired man. "Because of him, he tries batting me about with a paw. Move over here, now over there. Stop, go. And he doesn't let me play with Skyler."

A'idah swung her free hand out to point at the gray-haired man. "The old guy thinks he's better than the rest of us."

"Osamu is not old," Ytell said. "He's a little older than usual to react to Dark Matter for the first time, but it happens with the older ones sometimes and, yes, he is causing a problem."

Osamu gave a short bow to Alex, "Hello, Alex. I hope we can be friends. As you can see, my being here is not fitting into the alien's plans. I'm having trouble with the animals. I'm not much of an animal trainer."

"Animal trainer," Sabu hissed, standing up.

The blue bird burst into flight flapping about the room repeating over and over. "I don't need training! I don't need training!"

Zeghes dove through the air, swatting at Osamu with his tail, but Osamu ducked and Zeghes missed.

Alex jumped into the middle of the room and shouted. "We're all Earthlings!" Wheeling around he looked at everyone. "None of us are better than the others and all of us have been abducted by these aliens. We all have to work together."

A'idah hurried over and stood by Alex. "Alex is right. We need to calm down." They quieted down, somewhat. But then she said, "We don't order each other around."

Zeghes paused in his swimming through the air to look at A'idah. "I agree A'idah, it isn't good for females to order guys around. You'll need to remember that."

A'idah said, "That isn't what I'm talking about."

Sabu lashed her tail. "It isn't good for females to order guys around?"

Soon everyone was arguing. Their voices rose into yells as the argument grew. A sudden silence fell and everyone except Ytell collapsed to the ground. Ytell calmly walked around collecting bracelets from off everyone. "Now that you've experienced them, I'm collecting the civilization bracelets. The paralysis wears off quickly. Hopefully no one will need one replaced. You are all animals and we, the aliens Alex mentioned, consider you all people. As people you all have your own culture, but now you are part of my flock. You will learn to respect each other and work within the culture of your new life. The fact is, I lead this flock and will order you to do things. Your obedience is one very important part of this new culture. The penalty for not obeying can be death. Not because I would kill any of you. It is because there are going to be very dangerous experiences in this next year. We have only this one trial year to win the opportunity for you to receive your full nine years training, which means we will not have time to be careful.

"Now let me continue the introductions. But first, Zeghes, you need to be careful with your tail. If Osamu's head had been the ball you've enjoyed playing with, you could easily have hit it at least twenty feet. Human heads can't stand that kind of blow." Ytell pointed with a skinny arm, which reached out from under his wing, at a boy with dark skin and black, curly hair huddled over a foot long, black object. "This is Ekbal and he's investigating his latest source of curiosity. I think it's a scale."

Ekbal lifted the scale off the floor. Underneath the scale's bright yellow and orange shined in the light.

"Now if we can get his attention away from investigating his find, I will introduce him. Ekbal!" Ytell barked.

"What?" Ekbal asked, looking up to focus on Alex. "Oh, the new guy. Hi. What did you do?"

"What did I do?"

"I meant back on Earth before we were abducted," Ekbal said. "What strange thing happened?"

"Oh," Alex said, and after a moment's recollection related his story.

"Your karma is good. Maybe you'll help balance her karma," Ekbal said, pointing at A'idah.

A'idah scowled at Ekbal. "Regardless of what you think, standing up for what's right is good."

Ekbal spoke in a sing-song voice. "The great Swami Vivekananda said, 'You will not be punished for your anger, you will be punished by your anger.'"

Ytell interrupted. "If you listen to me and work hard, all of you will do things you can only imagine at this time," Ytell said, continuing to introduce the flock. "You've already met A'idah and Zeghes. Over here, being unusually quiet is this hyacinth macaw, Skyler."

"My turn to talk," the beautiful, blue bird said. "Oh, ok. Hi, Alex. It's good to see you. Alex, you've nice black hair. Hold your arm out."

He flew to Alex. When he had landed on Alex's arm, Skyler's tail reached down past Alex's hips. Skyler tipped his head to look at Alex. "Nice strong arm for having been so sick. Welcome to our flock. I hope you are good for flock. I better go back to my perch."

"Over here we've Peter," Ytell said, pointing back to a corner. "He is our disbeliever."

An angry man Alex hadn't noticed before leapt to his feet as if on a spring.

"I believe in God," snarled Peter, an intense-looking man with dark brown hair. "What I don't believe in is that I'm doing magic. Magic is of the devil."

Alex remembered hearing magic was of the devil. "Ytell, what's this magic?"

Ytell looked at Alex. "Dark Matter doesn't make anyone do supernatural things. It's all natural. Some animals and plants become able to do new things. Some we can explain and some we can't. Certain things will happen without you thinking about it. Others you'll have to work at. We call both

41

types of things vapuc. It isn't magic, but vapuc can be considered magical or miraculous until it is understood. How some religions react to vapuc can cause a problem for accepting people who react to Dark Matter. Dark Matter by itself is not evil, but deems will come with the Dark Matter and they are evil."

Peter pointed his finger at Ytell. "You admit what you are doing is magical and therefore magic or evil."

Ytell ruffled his feathers. "Peter, you are jumping to conclusions. I said magical in the sense of mysterious. Natural forces we don't understand are magical by that definition. Enough of this discussion."

"Ytell? What are deems?" Ekbal asked.

"They are many different kinds of creatures," Ytell said. "They live wherever there is enough Dark Matter. All of them except one, the L'fantoms and their young L'fantomys, will enjoy trying to cause you as much pain as possible. The L'fantoms work with us to find our students. We are going to teach you how to protect yourself and others from deems. Today is just a small step toward that goal. If you obey me, I might have enough time to teach you what you need to know. Hopefully you can learn to work together. Otherwise deems will kill you. If one of the many other dangers we face doesn't do it first."

Ytell looked around at everyone. "And as part of that small step, everyone follow me to the Hall of Flight." Ytell walked out of the room.

Still feeling the anger radiating out from Peter, Alex hurried over to Osamu. "Are you a Japanese astronaut?"

"Yes. Now you are astronaut. Its significance has changed. I'm just Osamu."

"My aunt knew you. She saved your life."

Osamu bowed to Alex. "Your aunt was special. If there is ever anything I can do for you, let me know. I'll never forget her sacrifice."

The talk about his aunt bothered Alex. It made him think of someone else, but he couldn't quite remember who. Alex walked beside Osamu. "Understanding animals is amazing."

"Yes. Sabu doesn't say much and she likes to play rough. She gave me some nasty scratches. The animals act like kids trying to act like adults. I try to help Ytell with the animals... I guess I need to start referring to them as people. Those people aren't very happy with me. How do you get along so well with Zeghes?"

"What reason do they have to be happy with you or with this situation?" Alex asked. "They've been taken from the lives they understand. The way all of us were captured was pretty rough. I got lucky with Zeghes. He became my friend, or by his way of looking at it his pod member, because of my fight with Ytell."

Passing through a doorway, Alex swayed, dizzy, and then reached a hand out to the wall to regain his balance. The ceiling, its height above him made his mouth drop open in wonderment. He looked over the edge of the floor and quickly stepped back. *This is like an indoor stadium, except with flat walls, platforms instead of rows of seats, and much bigger.*

They stood way above the ground. In the distance, he saw similar platforms jutting out from the walls on both sides of the hall and creatures floating in shimmering spheres. A huge purple crystal hung from the ceiling. Ytell's voice interrupted Alex's gazing at the crystal. He didn't understand what Ytell said. *What are bubble platforms? Yellow circles on them create bubbles?* He heard Ytell finish with, "Everyone, find a yellow circle to stand on."

Alex moved toward a yellow circle to his left, but Sabu jumped on it. He had to go to the back of the flock to find an unoccupied yellow circle. Stepping onto the yellow circle he listened to what Ytell said, trying to understand.

Ytell nodded at his flock. "Stay still until the bubble forms. These are special bubbles used to determine the individual's ability to react to Dark Matter. The more you react to Dark Matter, the better you'll be able to control the movement of your bubble with your thoughts. Not everyone can use these bubbles, but anyone can use normal bubbles."

"What's the red circle?" Ekbal asked.

"It's broken," Ytell answered.

Alex watched bubbles grow up from the circles until they surrounded the individuals. *What's that odd tingling sensation?* Looking down he saw a bubble rapidly encase him.

"Osamu, what's happening?" Alex asked, with trepidation born not from the tingling, but from a sense of foreboding.

"It's okay."

Alex brushed off Osamu's assurance and looked around, sure something bad was about to happen. The look of the bubbles made him grin despite his concern. Each had an iridescent sheen, just like soap bubbles. The floor of the bubbles didn't curve as he expected. Instead they were flat, providing a comfortable place to stand. Inside his bubble, Zeghes soared into the middle of the hall. Others floated up and moved slowly away.

Shouting interrupted the scene and drew Alex's attention.

Peter held his hands up as if to ward off the walls of his bubble. "Protect me from this evil, Lord! Keep these demons from me! With thy power, these demons have no control over me!"

Over the yelling came Ytell's firm voice, "You have been identified as someone who through a natural force, not a spiritual force, does many things mostly unexplained by our science. I don't have time to waste. This will prove if Dark Matter affects you."

With that, Ytell partially opened his wings, which then spanned twenty feet. A mighty beat of his wings caused a gust of air to push Peter's bubble over the edge of the platform, and it fell. Everyone heard a short scream. A moment later, Peter in his bubble rocketed back up.

"What have you done to me?" Peter sobbed. "I thought you were interested in what I told you about God, but then you did this."

"I did enjoy listening to you," Ytell said, "but you need to listen also."

The flock bobbled, soared, or at least gently moved through the air in their bubbles, except for Alex. It wasn't what happened to Peter that kept him standing still. *Something's wrong.*

"Come on, Alex. Just make your bubble move," Osamu said. "It responds to your thoughts."

"Come on, Alex. It's fun," A'idah said.

The swirling of the air had seemed to make his bubble move a little, and jumping up and down caused his bubble to bounce. Sweat beaded on his forehead at the thought of a solution. *I'll just run off and float, like everyone else.*

Alex charged forward in his bubble and off the edge. The sides of the wall passed by his eyes faster and faster. *Come on, bubble, float, rise, or soar.*

"Ahhh!" Alex started to yell. *I'm going to hit the ground.*

Zeghes in his bubble dashed below him and bounced into his. Alex fell against the side of the bubble. The bounces continued with Alex getting knocked around in the bubble. Finally, his bubble bounced back onto the platform. The bubble dissipated, leaving him sprawled on the ground at Ytell's feet.

That hurt. Why did I try that?

Ytell said, "Go stand out of the way by the entrance." He turned to Zeghes. "Thanks. If necessary, I would've caught Alex, but you used great initiative."

"No! I'm trying again," Alex said.

"Alex," Ytell leaned his head down toward him. "Fighting with me is a waste of our time."

Alex felt the tingling sensation start again. *Good, I'm not giving up.*

Ytell stared at Alex, his cruel beak lowering toward him. "I told you to go back to the entrance."

The bubble disappeared. Alex said in an accusatory tone, "You got rid of my bubble."

"I do not have time to figure out what's going on with you right now. Go stand by the wall."

Back stiff, Alex stalked reluctantly to the wall. He watched as the others moved about in their bubbles. As he watched his thoughts stewed within him. Why didn't his bubble do anything? Was this all a mistake? Would they take him back to Earth as a failure? He'd like to get to know A'idah better. He wanted to be part of this. At least he was healed. He couldn't believe that being healed was no longer so important.

"I'll teach you to spin me." Skyler's voice came from the middle of the hall, snatching Alex's attention. Sabu and Skyler had a game of tag going on. Sabu had just spun Skyler's bubble with a swat from a magically enlarged paw. As everyone watched, Skyler let Sabu close in behind him. It became evident he could move faster as he rolled up and over coming right behind Sabu.

With a, "See how you like this." Skyler clamped ahold of Sabu's bubble with what looked like an incredibly large bill and shook it.

Ytell said, "Skyler and Sabu just demonstrated an innate ability to do two forms of *vapuc*, illusion and force. Vapuc is not magic or a spiritual force of any kind. Vapuc is what we call the things you can do if you react to Dark Matter. When we get to the academy, you'll learn how force works. How they made the enlarged bill and paw appear still puzzles us."

Peter came close to Alex. "You're a lucky one, Alex. This evil has no grip on you." His voice rose, "I pray for my own release from this foul situation."

Stepping toward Peter, Alex said, "But this is a chance for us to help other people."

"How can you trust what these aliens say? You're a child. How can you understand? I'm a preacher, a man of God. I know what's right and wrong."

Zeghes soared up to them. "Leave Alex alone! You sound like Heyeze. He led many of my people to their death. He tried to tell them he was the source of truth, but he knew nothing. He was evil. I don't know much. But claiming you know what's right and wrong is just like Heyeze."

"Ha," Peter said. "Animals don't have philosophers. You're lying."

Zeghes charged Peter's bubble and yelled, "Begone!" With a shriek that faded in the distance, Peter's bubble ricocheted about the hall.

A'idah came up. "Good job, Zeghes. The other humans need to respect everyone. Hang in there, Alex. We'll get this figured out."

Ytell said, "Zeghes, I understand why you attacked Peter, but we can't fight each other. Consider this your only warning.

If you fight with each other, a civilization band will be put back on you. Now, everyone, head back to our common room. I'll meet you there."

Osamu said, "Ship, please give us a guide back to our rooms."

A ball of light materialized in front of the flock and bounced through the air toward the doorway they had come through earlier.

As the flock followed the guide, Osamu walked on the opposite side of Alex from A'idah. "Don't worry about your bubble experience. These aliens will figure out what's wrong."

"This is an incredible place," Alex said, as he looked at Osamu. "I hope I don't get sent back to Earth."

Osamu patted Alex on the back. "Saving those kittens proved you react to Dark Matter."

"Maybe my saving the kittens was a one-time shot."

"Stop questioning yourself," Osamu said.

Starting to hobble, A'idah took Alex's hand. "It doesn't matter if you react to Dark Matter or not. It doesn't change who you are. They better not try to send you back. I'll refuse to cooperate. They can lock me up in a cage or torture me. It won't do them any good."

From above, Zeghes nudged A'idah with his bill. "You're limping. We need to get you back to Gursha, so she can help you finish healing."

Skyler came flapping and dodging past them. "What a crazy flock this is. Flocks have to work together to survive. I need food. I'm so hungry."

Alex said, "A'idah, what's wrong? I thought you were cured."

A'idah grumbled in response. "Soon. Gursha told me to be patient. Supposedly, my nerves need more time to fully heal, until then I have to put up with this"

As they arrived at their common room, two stocky people and one of the kimley kids each pushing a cart loaded with food came into the room, from the other side. A huge ball of water filled with fish floated along behind the last cart. Alex found himself staring at the boy and his large lavender eyes with golden flecks drifting in the depths. The colors at his temples reminded Alex of the wings of butterflies. Alex didn't consciously notice, but in his mind quiet notes of a song tentatively began and then died.

One of the short men with a black beard said, "You're back just in time to eat. You should be aware another flock suffered food poisoning yesterday. Hopefully no one else has problems with the food." He chuckled and pointed at his barrel chest. "I'm Numbel." He pointed to a bald man with a pointed, white beard. "The grumpy one over there's Haal—."

Ekbal interrupted, "Are you two dwarves?"

Alex grinned. At first sight of the two men he too had thought of the fantasy people. *I wouldn't have asked such a —*

Numbel interrupted Alex's thoughts, and the boy's mouth dropped open at the answer. "We are dwarves, but not the creatures of your fantasy literature. Our name is just one of the strange coincidences of the universe. Our helper is Hhy. He and Haal will help you with your food."

Alex hadn't thought he could eat after failing to move his bubble. The news of food poisoning didn't help. Now however, smelling and seeing the food made his stomach growl.

A soft voice spoke up, "Be careful with the fruit. I think someone goofed. It might be too spicy for you, but Numbel was just joking about the food poisoning."

Alex looked for the speaker. It was Hhy. Alex smiled and the boy smiled back and then looked away. *Something about that boy is strange. Yeah, he's an alien.*

A'idah walked up to Alex. "He's one of those troublesome Soaley boys. Come over here. How does this water float in the air?"

Osamu stood examining the big ball of water with fish swimming in it. Tentatively he poked at it and waved his hands under it. "I would like to know too."

Alex racked his brain for an explanation. "In the space station, doesn't water make balls like this?"

Osamu looked appraisingly at Alex. "Yes, Alex. What are you thinking?"

"Well, we're on a space ship and yet we experience gravity. That means the aliens must have technology to control gravity. Couldn't they make the area of the ball have no gravity?"

"I knew you could tell me how the aliens did this," A'idah said.

Osamu raised one eyebrow and told Alex. "Very good, Alex. I think you are right. Oh, the things we will do on Earth with this technology."

While everyone ate, a creature floated into the room. Tentacles hung from a large translucent bulbous bag. It looked like a large jelly fish. Sabu left her food, crouched close to the floor, and eyes intent on the creature followed with her tail twitching behind her. It floated lower over some spilled drink and began to suck the liquid from the floor. Eyes wide, Alex stopped eating to watch. Just as Sabu pounced, the creature shot up into the air and squirted Sabu with a liquid. "Earth creature, you cannot hunt here. I will report this incident to your flock leader."

Ears flat against her skull Sabu jumped up onto a ledge. Alex started to laugh until he realized the seriousness of the situation for all the different Earthlings. *Are we going to be able to work with these aliens?*

Ekbal interrupted Alex's thoughts. "That fruit looks tempting to me." After gazing at it for a moment he walked over to the cart.

"Did you hear the fruit might be spicy?" Alex asked.

Ekbal paused, hand hovering over the fruit. "Yes, but it looks so good." He took an orange and green-striped one and popped it into his mouth.

"Hmm this tastes good, not too hot." His face turned red, and tears streamed down his face. "Oh, hot! Water, water!"

Hhy snatched a drink off a cart and hurried toward Ekbal who blundered about, waving his arms and calling for help.

Hhy ducked under one waving arm and dodged to the side. Ekbal blundered into the floating ball of water. Unfortunately, he tried to talk, and bubbles rose from his mouth. Gasping and choking, he ducked back out of the water. Hhy slipped a slender arm around him to support him. After Ekbal's breathing steadied, he took the drink and gulped the liquid down.

"Thanks. The fruit tasted wonderful. I wonder if a second one would be as painful."

When Haal and Hhy started picking up after the meal the flock jumped up, some to help, and others to eat a little more.

"Wait," Skyler said. "I want more nuts."

Sabu swatted playfully at Skyler's tail. "You'll get too fat to fly,"

Skyler knocked a bowl over spilling its contents across the floor, as Ytell entered the room.

Seeing Ytell, Skyler said, "It was Sabu's fault. She swatted me."

Alex didn't know how to read expressions on Ytell's avian face, but as Ytell looked at Sabu and Skyler it seemed to Alex he was exasperated.

"Peter won't be coming back," Ytell said. "Alex, come with me. We're going to Amable."

Alex's chest tightened. *Is this my last moment with the flock? Who's Amable?*

"Alex, we need to go." Ytell said impatiently.

Turning around to look at everyone, Alex choked out one word. "Bye." He avoided looking at A'idah. *I can't cry. Not in front of everyone.*

Zeghes leaped through the air, bumping Alex with his head. "Will he not come back? Shouldn't one of us go with him?"

A'idah hobbled to Alex and took his hand.

"Well, it does look like you have supporters. Only Alex comes with me.

"A'idah and Zeghes, on my world your type of loyalty is greatly valued. Also, my world is a very harsh place. My people discard young who fail. Regardless of what the decision is, I will bring him back here. In the future, I need all of you to trust me. My training methods will often seem like you are on your own, but I'll be watching out for you. You are my flock. I would die for you,"

Chapter Eight
What will be done with Alex

Meanwhile in Amable's office, Alex's fate was being discussed.

"No, no, no, we can't send Alex back to Earth," Amable said to Stick, the only other person in Amable's office. A faint tune recognizable as Ode of Remembrance emanated from the resting fish-plant.

Stick rubbed his chartreuse forehead. "But he doesn't react to Dark Matter. He won't be able to do any types of vapuc. Keeping him for the next year is a waste of resources. Let me show you the figures."

"And I'm telling you even if Alex doesn't react to Dark Matter, he'll be of use to the flock. If his flock develops as it should, they'll help deal with the threats to the academy. Alex's life will be in danger as a nonvapuc-able person, and his flock will have to learn to protect him," explained Amable. "That will be good for the flock, but I also hope we can find something Alex is good at."

"But sir, there's more. I checked with Gursha about Alex's sickness. She told me Alex isn't responding to treatment as he should. She doesn't think he'll recover from his illness. In fact, she suspects other aliens did something to him. Alex could be part of Maleky's plan for Earth. It would be just the thing he would do."

Amable said, "Of course Stick, and we can't forget the deception involved with Alex supposedly saving the kittens. He remembers saving the kittens, but he doesn't react to Dark Matter, except maybe sensing the future. Ergo, he couldn't have done vapuc in saving the kittens. The L'fantoms informed me the deems have certain types of crystals which

51

could have been used to fool them into thinking Alex reacted to Dark Matter. Someone wanted us to find Alex."

"It has to be Maleky," Stick said, wiping sweat off his forehead. "What are we going to do about Alex? I still think we should send him back to Earth."

Amable placed his arm around Stick. "There is an old saying, keep your friends close and your enemies closer. We are keeping Alex very close."

"Then you won't use the two Soaley kids to test him?"

"I don't see why not."

"But we don't trust them either."

"That's true," Amable said. "Having Alex and the kids together will let us keep an eye on all of them at the same time. Besides, the Weird suggested using the two boys for Alex's training and I trust him."

"Alex seems like such a nice boy," Stick said sadly. "Wouldn't it be better to send him back to Earth? Might we... have to... kill him?"

"You're letting your emotions get in the way of your logic. If Alex is an unwitting tool of Maleky, sending him back to Earth would be a death sentence. And I'm surprised at you for suggesting killing Alex. We don't kill people unless it is unavoidable to save others. Unlike Maleky, he destroys all who fail him. Besides, Mrs. Soaley took the rare action of sharing what she knew of the future just to make sure we wouldn't miss Alex in our search of Earth for creatures who react to Dark Matter."

"We still trust the adult kimleys?" Stick asked.

"Yes, as much as we trust anyone."

"Then we continue with your plan."

~**********~

Alex held onto A'idah's hand. *I don't want to leave.*

Zeghes glided right up to Ytell's beak. "I should go with Alex. He's still sick, and he might get abducted again."

Confused at his words, Alex looked at Zeghes. "How could I get abducted again?"

Zeghes hesitated and said, "Saying abduction was probably wrong. Our bodies were abducted the first time, but now I feel like who I am is being abducted. I mean... since I've been here, I've changed, and I'll never be the same again. My self is being abducted. Who knows what these aliens will do to you."

Ekbal came forward. "Wow, Zeghes. Dolphins do have philosophers, because you're one."

A'idah said, "I think it's good to change. I'm looking forward to learning how to protect myself and others. But there's another type of abduction. I've seen women fall in love and get married. I think falling in love is a form of abduction, but Alex doesn't need to worry about it. How would he fall in love with an alien?"

Alex stood with his mouth open, as he tried to figure out what to say, but overwhelmed by thoughts. *Falling in love with an alien? Ew, that sounds gross and crazy. And why does Zeghes' concern about changing bother me?*

Ytell reached a long, thin arm out from under his feathers to grasp Alex. "Okay, enough with all the talk. We have to go."

As Ytell pulled Alex after him, the group said their farewells.

"Good luck, Alex."

"If you see some nuts, bring some back."

"Remember to believe in yourself."

"Don't show fear, that's when the sharks attack."

~**********~

Walking away from the flock, Alex tugged his arm away from the raptor. Ytell still felt quite alien to him, and feeling the scaly hand on his arm was unsettling. As they walked, he glanced at Ytell. "Would you really die for me?"

"Yes. For us raptors, it's a matter of honor."

"My Aunt Debbie died saving others. Dying so others can live is the greatest sacrifice."

"That's partly why Amable and all of us are fighting to save worlds from deems. We're willing to give our lives for the battle."

Ytell and Alex stopped before a door. They heard a "Come on in," as the door slid open. A strange man with pink and violet hair, two tufts stuck out almost a foot from above his ears, hurried over to Alex. He grasped Alex's hand and shook it vigorously. "Ah, here you are, Alex, a fine young man. I'm Amable, and the last time I saw you, everyone was quite worried about you. It's wonderful to see you looking better. Obviously, Gursha has worked her miracles on you. How're you feeling?"

Alex choked back a laugh, as he gazed at the strange-looking man with large golden-brown eyes set in a pale face. Alex said, "Much better. It's been great getting healed. Gursha told me to come back again this—."

"She says you're doing marvelous," Amable said interrupting Alex. "She's going to check your progress and wants you to go through an exercise program. Your two personal trainers will meet you tomorrow. I've been so glad for how willing you are to do things. I presume you're willing to do this exercise program."

Alex shrugged his shoulders. *What things? What's he talking about?* "I guess. What is it?"

"Just some exercises," Amable said herding Alex and Ytell out of his office. "Glad you agreed to the program. The good news is you can rejoin your flock as soon as the training is over."

"Wait. Who are my trainers?"

"You'll meet them tomorrow. Goodbye."

The door shut in Alex's face. "Why wouldn't he answer me?" Alex asked Ytell.

Ytell squatted down to look Alex in the eye. "There's something he doesn't want to tell you. I'm sorry, but I don't know what it is."

Alex opened his mouth to respond and then shut it. *What do I say to this alien? How much are they not telling me or lying about?* He shook his head in confusion. "I better go see Gursha."

Ytell nodded his head. "And I better get back to the rest of the flock. No telling what they're doing."

For a moment Alex stood alone in the passageway, as the sound of Ytell's footsteps faded. *It's so quiet. Where is everyone?* Remembering the instructions for moving about in the passageways, he said, "Ship, please supply a guide to Gursha's clinic."

A bright bobbing light floated in the air, moved opposite the direction Ytell took, and waited for him. Alex shrugged trying to get rid of his nervousness and started down the empty passageways toward the clinic. Minutes went by with one empty passageway after another. A misty green cloud floated around a corner. Alex stopped, and stepped back warily watching the cloud. His guide light bounced to a halt.

"It's okay, Earthling," a feminine voice coming from the cloud said. "You don't need to be frightened."

"You didn't frighten me," Alex said, lowering his hands and unclenching his fists. "I was just startled."

The cloud floated along the hallway toward Alex, and he stepped to the side to let her pass him. She drifted beside him and then suddenly oozed through the air at him. With a gasp, Alex flattened himself against the wall. Laughter filled the air. Abruptly it stopped. The cloud swirled in the air to face down the hallway. She backed up. A multitude of thoughts whirled in Alex's head. *She's just teasing me. How can she seem to face somewhere? I don't see any eyes.* A last thought made Alex both want to run and look down the hall. *What frightened her?*

Alex looked down the passageway to see a translucent creature roughly eight feet tall and four feet wide. It stomped on thick legs toward them. Each step caused shivers of movement through the massive body.

In an urgent tone, the cloud girl said to Alex, "Go on. I'll keep the baby lepercaul from hurting you."

For a moment Alex stood still, until the other creature spoke in a voice which was a strange combination of babyish, deep, and threatening.

"I'm not a baby. And I just want to taste the earthling. I've heard they're tasty. Ha-ha-ha. I wouldn't hurt him... much. He-he-he."

Alex followed the cloud girls' advice and started walking down the hall, trying not to run, as his guide light resumed moving. *Everything's going to be okay. I'm not scared.*

At first, he continued to hear the conversation behind him.

"You aren't supposed to be out here. You —"

"I can too. Hymeron has some fun for me."

Looking around with wide eyes, Alex walked faster and faster. Until eventually, he ran gasping into the clinic. Gursha's boisterous voice greeted him. "Hello, Alex. Is someone chasing you?"

Alex looked at her. *I'm going to be okay. I just need to keep it together and not show how frightened I am.* "No. I... just didn't want to be late." *Deep breath and change the conversation* "Where's all of your medical equipment?"

"The holo fields are my equipment," Gursha said. "Less advanced technologies use a confusing amount of unsanitary medical tools. It's a wonder everyone in your hospitals doesn't die from infections. Now, lie down in this holo field."

Alex smiled at Gursha and did as she asked. His view of the room turned pinkish as the haze of the holo field surrounded him.

"Why's everything pinkish?" Alex asked.

"Pink haze shows the areas of illness or problems. That's what's coloring your view of the room. Now, I'm going back to my office, and I want you to lie still."

Lying still, Alex started to think about the strange creatures he'd met in the passageways. *The situation couldn't have been as bad as it seemed. What was it saying about Hymeron?* Alex closed the door on those thoughts. *Everything is going to be okay.* Next his mind wandered to Hhy. Something about the boy puzzled him. *What was it?* Then thoughts of A'idah crowded Hhy out of his mind. He understood A'idah. *She's so... I like spending time with her.* He laughed to himself. *I think I'm drawn to her because we're both human and she's just a couple of years younger than me. I can't wait to see her again.*

At that thought, he remembered his dad and a conversation with him back before his parents died. Anguish rose up with the memory. "Son, you're becoming a teenager. You're going to have new feelings and urges. Eventually, you'll be drawn to girls. Be careful about letting the feelings and urges control you. You've seen the wonderful relationship your mom and I have. If you wait until you're older to get serious about a girl, then you can build a relationship like we have. Don't play with a girl's feelings. Treat her with respect. In your heart and mind, you'll know what's right. But it can be very difficult to do what's right. Know your mom and I will always be there for you, and we'll be praying for you."

Except they aren't. Dad lied. Tears started to flow down Alex's cheeks. *I need their help. I miss them.*

At that moment, Gursha bustled in with Alex's dinner. "We're-Oh, Alex, what's wrong?" Gursha left the dinner to slip two hands under his shoulders, a third hand smoothed his hair back from his forehead, and the fourth hand held one of his hands.

Feeling like a baby, Alex leaned into Gursha. "I miss my folks."

"You'll see them in a year. We'll be taking you back for a visit."

"No. You don't understand. They're dead."

"Oh. Alex, it's good that you miss them. That means you love them. What do you believe about death?"

"My folks believed it was just a passage from this life to an eternal life."

Gursha looked into Alex's eyes. "What do you believe?"

"I don't know. When they died, I prayed to God, and I got comfort. But I don't really know what I believe."

"Alex, I've lost loved ones." Pausing to look away, Gursha added in a soft voice. "I've lost too many." Taking a deep breath, she looked back at Alex. "If you live life well you're going to lose people you care for, but if you never lived then you never had them to lose. You have to find comfort in positive things that keep you living and giving. Be careful. There are things that will comfort, but they'll diminish you. The good kind of comfort keeps us strong in here." Gursha said, taking a hand away from his forehead to hold it over

Alex's heart. "We have to be strong in there to help those still living."

"Thanks, Gursha," Alex said.

"You can come to me with your problems anytime," Gursha said. "Now, we're making some progress with your cure. Your prescription is to eat, exercise, rest, and repeat."

"Repeat?" asked Alex.

"Keep doing those three things until I tell you to stop," Gursha said.

"You mean when this is done, I won't have to eat or rest?"

"You know what I mean," Gursha said with a laugh. "Now eat this food, and get some sleep. Tomorrow will be a busy day for you."

"How long before I'm totally cured?"

The holo field lifted Alex into a vertical position, and Gursha engulfed one of his hands with her large hand. "Alex, most of the fatigue is gone, but there are some problems I'm having trouble getting rid of. You and I will beat this. The uncertainty is part of the journey."

After Alex finished eating and as he drifted off to sleep, he heard her whispering to herself, "I hope Alex can defeat this evil in him."

Briefly the message caught his awareness before sleep finished taking hold.

In the middle of the night Alex's hands groped for a non-existent weapon. His eyes popped open, and he looked around Gursha's barren clinic in the dim light. A dream about battling evil inside him still felt so real. He remembered his disappointment the evening before, when Gursha told him he was going to have to fight the illness for a while longer. Trying to force himself to feel better, he daydreamed about Zeghes and A'idah giving him his training. All the time, he wanted and hoped to fall back asleep and have better dreams. His worry about the illness morphed into wondering who or what would be training him. *I don't know any of these aliens, and I can't imagine understanding just how strange some of them are.*

Finally, his body relaxed and he drifted back off to sleep. In the morning, Alex's eyelids fluttered in his sleep. A smile tugged at his mouth. A flowery fragrance drifted about on a breeze blowing across a meadow filled with strange and yet beautiful plants. A figure stepped out of dark evergreens bordering the meadow and walked slowly toward him. She wore a brown robe and her long light-brown hair danced in the breeze. Streaks of blonde and red hair twinkled in the sunlight. She raised her face, and he saw emerald green eyes with long curly eyelashes. Leisurely she swayed closer to him. The red of her lips caught his attention as the full lips slowly curved into a smile. Alex's heart beat faster and he stepped forward. She demurely ducked her head to the side. A slender hand covered her smile, but Alex could tell she still smiled because of two dimples in her cheek. He felt the desire to brush his fingers lightly across the cheek, trace the jawline back to the firm chin, and touch her lips. *How exotic she is.* His breathing came faster. *Her jaw shouldn't be so long.* Alex froze and took a quick step back.

The girl dropped her hands and turned a pleading face toward him. *Her eyes are too big to be normal.* She lifted her hands and the robe slipped over her skin to show long graceful arms. "Don't be afraid. I love you." She paused, mouth slightly open, and Alex could see her sharp pointed teeth. *She's an alien.* He tried to scream, but nothing would come out. He tried to turn and run, except he had lost all control of his body. In growing terror he watched her coming closer. She lifted one hand to the side of his face and he felt it playing in his hair. In a sultry voice she whispered in his ear. "It won't hurt you, too much."

She slipped back and he watched her lips pucker for a kiss and felt his own responding for the contact. *I want to kiss her.* Then he was awake and gasping in the holo-field. "No. No. No. Gross. I do not want to kiss an alien."

Later as Alex ate breakfast, Gursha's voice interrupted his thoughts. He was startled by the change in her voice. She spoke in a very firm tone. "Alex, I need to talk to you about a problem some of you human-earthlings have, particularly you and a British boy. Many of your new experiences must be frightening to you, but Ytell, Stick, and I have noticed you are not acknowledging those fears. This actually gives them more power over you and will slow down your acclimatization and therefore your training. We can't have that. Your human psychologists are aware of the need to acknowledge fear and have some great therapy for progressing through fear, but we don't have time to give you therapy."

All the time she spoke Alex wanted to say something, but she wouldn't let him get a word in. Instead his thoughts stayed bottled up in his mind. *Of course like a British man. Just like that spy in those movies. I'm a guy. Guys don't get upset or really scared. I don't need therapy.*

"I put a drug into the drink you just finished."

Alex dropped his empty glass on the floor. "What?" He interrupted furiously. "You didn't warn me. I trusted y—"

"I'm sorry, but there isn't time. If you want to help save your world, just listen. For a little while the drug will get rid of the inhibitions you have about how you react. At the same time you'll analyze your own reactions."

Alex stepped back from Gursha. *I don't need to understand my feelings. I'm going to be like the British spy, calm, cool, and able to take care of anything.* He opened his mouth to argue more with Gursha. Only to be interrupted as a bald man with a holographic display surrounding him came into the room.

A surprised Gursha said, "Stick, what are you doing here?"

Stick stopped waving his hands through the transparent pages of information and pictures in front of him. "Gursha, I don't like what Alex's going to go through. It isn't right."

"Stick, long ago we decided we couldn't always like what we do. He'll be okay."

Gursha gave Alex a concerned look, and Alex looked back at Stick. Then, Alex caught a glimpse of two kimley kids behind the man.

What are they up to? They aren't going to— His thought was answered by the thin man falling. His long skinny arms waved in the air, as he frantically tried to save himself from falling. Pages flashed and changed within the holograph in response to the motions of his arms.

The humor of the scene bubbled up in Alex and a laugh escaped. "Ha, ha." *What am I doing laughing? Those kimley kids are terrible.*

Stick lay on the ground, moaning about lost work and kimley kids. Alex and Gursha ran across the room and gently began helping him to his feet.

Amable walked into the room, dragging the two kimley kids behind him. "Are you all right Stick?"

At first Stick didn't answer. He let Gursha hold his face against hers as she whispered to him, until he pushed away from her to face Amable. "No. I'm not all right. Thanks to those two troublemakers, I just lost months of paperwork."

"Months?" Amable asked in disbelief raising a single bushy eyebrow.

"Okay, days. I thought you were going to do something about them terrorizing me."

"I'm giving Hhy and Hymeron the job we talked about. Also, if I hear of them causing more problems, they will be confined to their quarters."

"Great, just great and if no one wants to listen to my opinions, I'll just go to tech support and try to get my files recovered."

Amable said, "Go ahead and good luck."

Before Stick left, Alex spoke up. "Your nose, it's blue."

"Of course it's blue," sputtered Stick. "Whenever it gets hurt it turns blue. That's normal."

"Yes, normal," Alex said in a flat voice. Unknown to him, his subconscious cried out, "Julia isn't normal! Remember what happened! Remember Sammy!" Another voice in his mind said, "His subconscious is fighting me?"

Amable looked at the two kimleys. "This is Alex. Remember what I told you about behaving." Amable looked back to Alex. "Hhy and Hymeron are your trainers."

Alex barely noticed Amable's introductions. Something about Stick's blue nose still distracted him.

"Alex, did you hear me?" Amable asked. "These two boys, Hhy and Hymeron, are going to give you training and exercise."

"What?!" Alex stepped back, accidently activating a holo-field. The ground fell away. Alex screamed and the two kimleys laughed, while Alex waved his arms and legs about in a comical struggle. He cut the scream off and glared at them.

Breathing deep, he turned a pleading look at Amable. "I'm still trying to get used to being in a strange place with aliens, and you're going to stick me with them?"

"Yes, Hymeron and Hhy Soaley. They're brothers."

The kimleys stepped forward. They both wore baggy, grey pantaloons. The taller one, who had on a chartreuse vest over a fuchsia long sleeved shirt, grinned at him. The other sneered, and said, "You're funny. Could you wave your arms and legs about again?"

For a second Alex closed his eyes. He remembered how to get out of a holo-field and stepped to the ground. Trying not to sound desperate, Alex said, "But they're just little kids."

The taller one, Hhy, stood up straight and stomped up to him. Alex wanted to back away, but couldn't because of the holo-field behind him. Hhy tipped his head to look him in the eyes. The top of his head came up just short of Alex's chin. "I'm not that much shorter than you, so don't call me a little kid."

Alex found himself staring into big, lavender eyes with little golden flecks drifting in the depths. Unbeknownst to him a tune gently started up in his mind and died away.

"Have fun. I'll see you later." Amable's ear tufts gently waving, he made his escape from the room.

Amable's leaving shook him free from those eyes. "Wait! Come back! Don't leave me with them."

Chapter Nine
Trouble and Danger

Hymeron laughed and said, "If you're done eating, let's go."

Alex checked his shoes before looking at the kimleys. Hhy looked back at him and Alex avoided looking into those strange eyes. He turned to Hymeron and seeing the smaller boy's expression, Alex swallowed as he imagined how bad these kids were going to treat him. "Where're we going?"

"To give you some exercise," Hhy said, walking away with a laugh.

Alex ground his teeth. *He's saying that as if I'm a dog they're taking out for a walk.* Reluctantly following the kids, he heard Gursha say in a quiet, troubled tone, "Good luck. The drug will take effect soon."

Alex almost turned around and ran back when Hymeron chuckled. Resolutely he continued on. *I must be calm.*

When the smaller kimley said, "Careful you don't go down that hall."

Naturally, Alex had to look. At first, he didn't see anything until a skittering sound caused him to look up. A three foot wide spider on the ceiling raced toward him and then stopped. Eyes wide, Alex stood staring and screamed, "Aaah!"

After the initial surprise he continued talking to himself gradually getting quieter and quieter. "A huge spider, I'm going to be frightened. I don't want to be frightened. Wait, I'm not really frightened as much as I thought, just a bit scared."

The spider backed up, dropped to the floor, waved one leg at him, and left. Finally, Alex managed to move on past the forbidden hallway.

Other less frightening, but still strange creatures walked, floated, and flew past them as they walked along. Alex continued talking to himself, as each new experience startled him less than the last. *It's really no worse than some experiences on Earth. Everything's just stranger here. None of these aliens want to hurt me.* Alex walked around a corner after the kimleys and noticed this long passageway looked the same as an earlier one. Alex opened his mouth to ask a question when someone just a little shorter than him stepped out of a doorway and into the hall. The person was covered in a form fitting, brown robe with a cowl shadowing the face. Alex stopped and gave her his winningest smile. *What am I doing? How do....* He realized the robe hugged the figure approaching him and he answered his own question. *But I didn't decide to stop and smile. At least I'm no longer saying my thoughts out loud.* Out of nowhere he felt a compulsion to hold and kiss the female creature.

With a slim hand she reached up and pulled the cowl back. A beautiful girl, about his age grinned at him with double dimples in each cheek. With a sigh of relief Alex said, "Hi."

A flowery fragrance drifted about, relaxing him. The girl lifted one arm straight up and then her other arm straight up. The robe slid across her skin to reveal long slender arms. Suddenly Alex realized he was copying her. He tried but couldn't pull his arms back down. Slowly at first and then faster and faster he started turning in one spot, until dizzy and staggering he stopped. The mesmerizing girl stepped closer and slowly leaned toward him. In a husky voice she said, "I bet you think I'm attractive."

Alex agreed, but he wanted to be anywhere but here. *She's not human. She's an alien.* Instead, against his own will he found himself puckering up for a kiss. *No. No. No. Gross.* She puckered up and leaned against him. Breathing heavy, her hands explored his back. Quietly she said, "Silly human, so easy to control."

Alex stared at her, wanting the kiss. At the same time he screamed in his head. *No. No. No. She's an alien, gross.* Still he was terribly distracted by her leaning against him. He'd never had a girl pressed against him, and it was very disconcerting. *Kiss me*. Then he noticed her teeth were not just white and even, but also pointed and sharp looking. As he stood all puckered up for a kiss he didn't really want, Alex heard Hhy say, "What are you doing working with a winkle? You know how cruel they are."

Alex didn't understand the rest of the kimley conversation, as the girl tipped her head and bit him on the chin. With a gasp at the pain, he managed to step back against the wall. She licked her lips. "So you can fight back. I could have fun with you."

The girl stepped toward him and Alex slid along the wall. She held her arms out and he struggled not to step into her embrace. Another voice, a deep and strangely babyish voice, said, "Me, my turn to have fun with the human."

Alex looked and saw lumbering toward him the same creature the cloud girl helped him escape. Its words came back to him. "Hymeron has some fun for me."

Instinctively, Alex retreated from the large creature and bumped up against the girl. She slid an arm around him. "If you stand still, I won't let him hurt you, too much," she whispered in his ear. Alex didn't know what to do or what he could do. He felt a hand playing in his hair, meanwhile the gelatinous being reached one big arm out, and a burning pain came as its hand reached his chin. Alex opened his mouth to scream. He could see the red of his blood flowing in a trickle through the big creature's arm. Then a furious voice interrupted the scene. "Enough! Leave my flock member alone!"

Released, Alex fell to his knees. The gelatinous creature and the deceptively beautiful girl hurried away to vanish back through a door. Gasping at the experience Alex looked back up the hallway to see Ytell.

Ytell ruffled his feathers and with cold fury said, "Hymeron, you do not want to be in trouble with me. Take Alex to the *Weird* room. Now."

Alex looked back at the kimleys. Hhy's normally pale face looked even more pale, but Hymeron's face looked red and when he spoke Alex could hear the anger and frustration in his petulant answer to the interruption. "Okay, don't get your feathers all fluffed up. I was going to stop them. Come on Alex."

After a moment, Alex pushed off from the floor and looked back to thank Ytell for saving him, but his flock leader had gone. *I don't want to follow these two menaces, but what choice do I have?* Grudgingly, he admitted to himself he had to go with them. *From what I've seen in this walk, there are dangerous aliens around me.* He clenched his teeth as he made a vow to himself. *I'm going to pay these kimleys back for all the pain and torment they've caused me.*

At first Alex kept up with his tormentors, but eventually the adrenalin fueled energy faded. The trauma of his time following these two horrible people kept him quiet with his own thoughts. One thought refused to go away. The memory of the alien girl pressed up against him as he went to kiss her. He found himself fascinated by the memory even as he remembered the pain and revulsion. *Ew, this is gross and crazy.* Around a few more corners and he noticed a door which looked familiar. His anger wouldn't let him stay quiet. "Hey, you two, isn't that the same door we went past earlier? At this rate, when I arrive at wherever you're dragging me I'll be too tired to exercise."

"It's only been about thirty minutes," Hhy answered. He continued talking to Hymeron. "Although he's right, we should stop going in circles and get him to the Weird room."

Hymeron looked at both of them. "Oka—"

The door opened and a familiar translucent head looked out into the hall. The creature spoke interrupting Hymeron. "Hi. Humans do taste good."

Hymeron asked, "Where's Twarbie? She's supposed to take you back to your wild space."

The baby laughed. "She leaned against the wall and started twirling her hair with a finger. I told her she needed to take me back. she just said I think I like that boy. Then I thought about the human. I wanted to eat him."

Everyone stood still for a second and Hymeron said, "Your job's over and you're supposed to return to your wild space."

"Don't want to." The baby lepercaul whined. In a deeper, more confident tone he said, "I'm going to eat the human."

Hymeron retreated a step. Blusteringly he said, "You can't do that."

Alex shuffled backward as he tried to follow the conversation. *She likes me? What's its wild space?* The lumbering giant stepped out into the hall. In response Alex prepared to run.

Hhy whispered to him. "Start walking away." Hhy stepped toward the baby even as Hymeron backed up. In a calm voice, Hhy said, "If you try to eat the human, your parents will be mad at you and take away your favorite foods."

A giant hand reached out toward Hhy. She flinched but stood still and said, "You don't—"

The baby spoke over her voice. "I've heard my parents talking. They don't care about anybody else. Only Lepercauls matter to us. I think I'll find out how you taste too."

The lepercaul lunged at Hhy in a surprisingly fast move for the creature, but Hhy ducked. The lepercaul's arm swung into and past the kimley's head. Smoke rose from Hhy's head, hair fell, and he screamed, "Run!"

Alex paused for a second, worried about the kimley, but Hhy dodged away from the baby and ran toward Alex. In a moment all of them were racing down the hallway followed by the thundering sounds of pursuit.

Hymeron caught up to Alex and passed. "Follow me. He can't run as fast as us. We'll get away."

Hhy yelled at Hymeron. "Call Ytell about the wild baby."

Hymeron yelled back. "I got ahold of Twarbie, the winkle. She was supposed to return the baby to its wild."

Alex started falling behind Hymeron. Even as he raced away from the hungry baby, he noticed another thing he knew nothing about. *How are they getting ahold of people?* Hhy paced beside him. The kimley said, "Can't you go faster?"

Alex shook his head and gasped. "No... too... tired."

Hhy shouted at Hymeron. "We need another plan! The baby's going to catch us!"

They can survive. Alex said, "Leave..."

"Go faster," Hymeron shouted back.

"me..."

"Alex can't!"

"behind."

"I'll open a Utility portal!"

A swirling pattern formed quickly on the wall, widening to reveal a large hole. Hymeron dove through it. "Hurry up," He called out to Alex and Hhy. "Hopefully he's too big to follow us."

The thumping footsteps drew nearer every second. Alex turned his head to look at Hhy. *I'm not going to make it.* A hand grabbed the back of his clothes. With a pull and a shove he felt Hhy helping him dive through the hole. Tumbling he came to a stop on top of Hhy.

"Get off me, you big lump."

Quickly Alex pushed himself up. One hand was on a warm, mostly naked back.

A muffled, very angry exclamation came from Hhy. "Hey!"

Hymeron said, "Hurry up, you two. The baby's trying to get through the hole."

Alex quickly stood to his feet. In the light coming from the hole behind him he could see the tattered shirt, a quick flash of green, and a long red streak down Hhy's back. Alex reached down to help, but Hhy rose to his knees and scrambled across the floor. Following the example, Alex hurried across the floor. He found himself stumbling. Creatures wriggled across the floor and voices rose in complaint. "Hey, watch where you're going."

"What are you doing in here?"

Alex didn't recognize any of the voices. He gasped out an apology to the snakes and Hhy. "Sorry. The back... of your clothes... is all ripped... and I think you're bleeding."

Hhy's furious voice cut through the others. "Don't look at me. Keep moving. It can reach through the hole. You're too close to the opening."

Trying to be careful Alex moved farther from the portal. *What were those things?* This new passageway was only dimly lit, and besides the new creatures, objects, which he didn't recognize, leaned against the wall.

A big thump, followed by a whining voice signaled the baby's attempt to get through the portal. "Stop running. I'm hungry. Oh, maybe I could eat these things."

Alex looked back and in the light shining through the portal could see the baby had made it into the utility hall. His arms reached down, sparks zapped up from the snake things. Alex asked, "What... are they? Shouldn't we try to help them?"

Hhy tugged on his arm. "Come on, we've got to keep going. The Zorms won't distract it for long. They're more mechanical than flesh and won't let it eat them. They've been exploring the ship... since after the slaves rebelled against the ship's original owners..., deems. They also help with the ship's maintenance."

Something moving to the side caught his vision. *It's a reflection.* Now that Alex's eyes were getting used to the dimmer light, he could make out crystal-like things leaning against the wall. The sounds of the battle faded as they moved on.

Hhy said, "Be careful. We don't want to break these crystals. Some of them only deems know how to grow."

Catching his breath, Alex slowed. Breakable things? And he'd led the baby here? *What a crazy place and crazy aliens. I hope I don't need to remember what these snakes are called.* A colorful, pulsating glow came from around a corner. They went around the bend and stopped. Hymeron stood still in front of them. Alex gazed in wonder. A coruscating glow of different colors came from a forest of crystals.

Hymeron waved at them. "Come on."

Carefully they walked in-between the crystals. More of the snakes slithered about. Alex reached out to touch a crystal and Hhy slapped his hand away. "Don't touch them."

Alex said, "They look alive."

Hymeron said, "They are. We're in a secret garden. I've procured things for their experiments. So, they're okay with us being here, but don't tell anyone else about this. The Zorms hold grudges and you don't want to find out how they get even. If we damage these crystals, I'd either do what they said or disappear like my cousin."

Hhy said, "Uh, oh."

A familiar thumping sound grew louder. Hhy grabbed Alex by the hand again. "Run."

Hymeron shouted. "Come on you two! We've got to get out of here."

Hhy stopped tugging on Alex. Instead he wrapped a strong arm around Alex's back and supported him as they continued on. "It's no use. We can't outrun it. This time, Hymeron, you've really gotten us into bad trouble. You need to call Ytell or Amable for help."

"No, we can't call them from here." Hymeron's words snapped out of him. "This'll work. When this portal opens get through it quickly. It won't stay open long. Just don't break any crystals."

What's this kid talking about now? Whatever. It better work. A delicate blue and white crystal sprouted from the floor in front of him. Alex lifted his foot to step over it. A shimmering in the air caught his attention. In a second, the shimmering spread in a circle leaving a view of the normal passageway in the middle.

"Jump!"

Hhy pulled at Alex and he jumped feeling a tug on his trailing foot. A sharp snap and then he was tumbling on the hallway floor with the kimleys. By the time he got up, both the kimleys stood waiting by a door. Alex looked back the way they'd come to see a blank wall. "Where's the baby?"

Hymeron said, "The baby? You mean the terror. If it didn't break any crystals, then Twarbie will find it and get it back to its wild. If not.... Well.... The Zorms took care of it."

Hhy opened the door and entered. "Hymeron, use your AI to ask the Weird about healing my AI and me. Also I need some new clothes. Never mind, the Weird heard me without my AI working."

Hymeron stepped into the room calling back to Alex. "If you have any energy left, we can start your training."

For a moment, Alex stood outside in the hall. *They keep dragging me all around, and I've got so many questions I want answered, plus I'm too worn out to exercise.* Following them into a barren room, Alex said, "Uh, there's nothing in here." The walls, floor, and ceiling were white.

"Start running," Hymeron said, "unless you're already wimped out?"

"Where to?"

"That wall."

"Ha. The wall. Right." *I can do a few strides.* Alex took a couple of strides, expecting to stop at the wall. Except with each stride the wall didn't get any closer. In the background, he heard one of the kimley boys laughing at his surprise.

"What's going on?" he asked in amazement, as he continued running.

Alex stopped after half-a-dozen seconds. With his hands on his knees, he asked between pants, "Why... do I... never... get closer... to the wall?"

"This is a special place in many ways," Hymeron said. "It's called the Weird. The Weird isn't the name of this room as much as it is the artificial intelligence running this room. You're going to stay in this room until your training is done. It'll provide everything you need until you leave. Look at what it did for us."

Alex turned around and stared, open-mouthed at seeing Hhy relaxed in a chair, holding a tall, cold drink. A pink holo-field surrounded his head and already his white hair was growing back. A variety of snacks covered a small table between him and where Hymeron rested in a chair.

"Where did all that come from?"

"The same place as your chair," Hymeron said, snickering at Alex as another chair appeared beside theirs.

"Actually, sweaty as you are, I bet instead of a chair, you'd enjoy a shower," Hhy said grinning.

"That would feel good. Where is it?" Alex looked around getting a feeling something not good was going to happen. "What are you grinning about?"

A drop of water hit his head. Looking up, he saw a small dark cloud. Rain poured down onto his upturned face. Stumbling, he tried to get away, but it followed him. Inspiration directed him to stumble toward the kimleys. *I'll see what happens when I take this rain to them.* It stopped when he approached Hhy.

"Great, guys. Now how about some dry clothes?" Alex asked, laughing.

Giggling, they pointed to a door. Alex cautiously approached the door. It didn't take him long and he returned wearing dry clothes.

After lunch and a nap for Alex, Hhy and Hymeron took turns setting Alex up for pranks. Alex had a miserable afternoon. It finished with another run at the wall, except this time he ran into the wall and crumpled onto the floor, moaning in pain.

Through the agony fury filtered, until he pushed himself up. "You guys knew that was going to happen! I've had it with you two."

Panting and weaving, Alex chased the kids, until the floor turned slippery, his feet went out from under him, and he crashed limply onto the floor. A large, soft pillow appeared under his head just before he landed. In a second, he'd fallen asleep.

Later, Alex woke to the sound of a fountain. *Ah that's nice. Wait I'm in the Weird. Is there a real fountain?* He opened his eyes to check it out and saw—. In terror, he scrambled to his knees backing away. *It's that girl. The wi... the whatever.* Alex stopped moving as he painfully slammed into something. The winkle girl who had controlled him earlier and bitten him sat on the ground. She was dressed in a loose-fitting shirt and pantaloons. At his frightened response, she jumped to her feet. "I'm sorry—."

Before she could finish, Alex jumped to his feet and tried to back up more only to fall into the fountain with a splash. Holding his breath, he struggled, flailing his arms and legs about in the water. Her laughter bubbled through his frantic noises. *It's shallow.* Angry and feeling foolish, Alex relaxed and stood up. The water only came to his thighs. Warmth traveled up his neck and face at his embarrassment.

The girl quickly closed the distance. "Let me help you."

Leaning over she grasped Alex's arm. *What's she doing?* Instinctively, he jerked his arm back. Even as he desperately backpedaled away, he saw her eyes go wide. *They're so big.* Almost going over backward, he saw her trying to catch herself, but she fell forward into the water with a splash. The water sprayed up adding to the water still running off him. Panting as he steadied himself with one hand, Alex watched the girl. She didn't flounder about. In a moment she stood. The water ran smoothly off her body splashing down around her. Alex's mouth fell open at the sight. Her clothes were plastered against her.

In a rush the girl said, "Dry clothes on me, please."

In the blink of an eye, her wet clothing had been replaced with dry, except the pantaloons were still wet from her thighs down. "Will you listen to me, please? I'm sorry for what happened earlier."

"You forced me to spin around like a fool."

"Yes, it's called Controlling Animals. You'll learn it's a form of vapuc. My people are very good at it. I was part of Hymeron's plans. I—"

Even more indignantly Alex said, "You bit me."

She smiled and two dimples showed up on each cheek. "It was fun playing with you."

A frown crossed her face and the dimples melted away. Alex started to reply. *I wish she would smile more. She's so cute. Eck.* He shook his head.

The girl gave him a rueful grin. "I'm sorry, but I'm not very good at apologizing. I've never done it before."

Alex clambered out of the fountain's pool as he said, "Really?"

Gracefully she stepped over the edge.

He looked up and copying what she'd done said, "I could use some dry clothes too, please."

A voice, Alex presumed it was the Weird, said, "Here you go."

A shirt and pantaloons appeared in the air to fall on his face. He sputtered grabbing them from his head. What made it worse was hearing her chuckle at him.

Clearing her throat, she said in a matter of fact voice, "We Winkles are taught at a very young age to be tough and cruel. I was given a little pet as a very young girl. My mom encouraged me to pet it and cuddle it. I learned to love it. Then

I was forced to slowly torture it to death as a sacrifice to our God."

Alex noticed the girl's pantaloons were soaked all the way up her thighs and clung quite appealingly to her. Trying not to stare, holding the dry clothing awkwardly, and unsure of what to do, he said, "That's terrible."

For a moment, she looked back at him as different emotions chased across her face before he could recognize them. "It was terrible. That and many other things have made my life a living hell. Also, I was taught how to appeal to males, to make them easier to control. Dry pantaloons please and put his dry clothes on him."

Instantly Alex had on the dry clothes and was dry himself. Embarrassment and next anger began to grow. *She asks for forgiveness and then she does this?* He opened his mouth to speak.

The girl held her hand up. "No. I didn't get wet on purpose. I recognized the situation and tried to take care of it. What can I do for you to accept my apology?"

Confused and really uncertain, Alex hesitated. "What's your name?"

"Twarbie."

"Okay, Twarbie. Why do you want to apologize to me? Why didn't you just go off and continue your horrible life, torturing and sacrificing?"

Tears began to flow down her cheeks. "I don't want that life. I want to be different. If I tried this outside here and another Winkle saw me, then I'd be tortured and maybe sacrificed. All Winkles must serve our God or be killed."

Alex froze. *She's... She's... She's terrible..., but she's hurting. I don't think she's faking, but what do I know in this place. The religion of her people sounds terrible. Do I tell her of religions we have on Earth?* He took a step toward her. "Your life does sound terrible. On Earth we have many different religions and most allow people to choose for themselves how they want to live. The God my folks served sent his son to die for us, so we could be saved and know the depth of his love for us. That's quite different from what you've known. I was raised to try and help others." He paused, realizing her risk and said, "I won't tell anyone. Did Hymeron or Hhy see you come in here?"

Through sniffles, Twarbie said, "No."

"Okay, then leave the Weird and find me later. Give me some time to get to know you. We can try to be friends. Maybe I can find a way to help you and I'll forgive you."

"No. I don't want to leave the Weird, but I'd like to have a friend."

"What?"

"You don't understand this situation. You're in a time bubble. It means you have months to get stronger and learn. In the meantime just a day passes for your flock. While Hhy and Hymeron are with you, I'm going to stay in a secret room the Weird created for me. Please help me... be different."

A voice interrupted. "Twarbie needs to go. The kimley's are getting suspicious."

"I'll do it. Go."

"Okay, pretend to be asleep."

Chapter Ten
Twarbie

Alex ran to the pillow and lay back down. *How am I going to keep Twarbie a secret? This just keeps getting crazier. I wonder what happened to the terrible baby.* In a moment he heard the boys talking. He kept his eyes shut and listened.

"Remember what I said, we're going to treat him better," Hhy said.

Hymeron said, "I wasn't that hard on him. I still think you're overreacting because you're a g—."

"Hush," Hhy hissed. "He might be awake."

Hhy walked over to Alex and nudged him. "Alex, wake-up."

"What?" Alex asked. *What did Hymeron start to say about Hhy?*

"We'll have a snack and talk about your training," Hhy said.

Alex said, "I'm too sore to eat."

"Okay," Hhy said.

Alex suddenly became aware of tantalizing odors and sat up. "What are you guys eating?"

"Here's a bowl for you," Hymeron said.

Alex eagerly reached for the bowl. Suspicion stopped him. He paused looking intently into Hymeron's face. "Is it safe for me to eat?"

Hhy snatched the bowl from Hymeron and grasped a spoon that materialized in midair. He stirred the contents of the bowl and took a bite. After swallowing, he said, "It's a little spicy, but safe."

Alex took the offered food, shoveled some into his mouth, and mumbled his thanks.

In a voice filled with a surprising amount of concern, Hhy asked, "How's your face?"

"Sore," Alex said, feeling a little revived by the hot and spicy food, but still annoyed at the boys. "What's with you two? Do you have to do so many stupid things?"

In a petulant voice Hymeron said, "But we didn't do very many."

Alex glared back. "The small rainstorm was kind of funny. Making small, round rocks fly at me hurt. The pit that opened up in the floor scraped my legs pretty bad." Pointing at his bruised face and cuts on his arm, Alex added, "That doesn't cover the crazy time I had just getting to this room. I can go on."

"I thought it was funny," Hymeron said.

Alex pointed at his bruises and cuts. "Look at my face. Does that look funny?"

Hymeron glared back at Alex until he finally looked away. When Alex turned to Hhy, the tinkling notes of a wind chime played in his head, growing stronger, but he still didn't notice them.

Hhy said, "I'm sorry. I got a little carried away with some of the pranks. I never wanted you to get hurt, but you can't understand what it's like being a kimley."

"A little?" Alex asked with a bitter laugh. "I don't care about your problems. They still don't give you an excuse to torture me or mistreat others." *Boy I can relate. When I thought I was dying, I was a pain to be with. It seems like there was one person who cared about my problems and understood. I just can't remember who it was. I still think they should pay at least some for what they've done.*

"We—I didn't mean to hurt you," Hhy said. "The Weird has controls to prevent anyone from dying, and it can heal you just like it healed me and my AI."

"Why are you caving in?" Hymeron asked Hhy. Looking back at Alex, he added. "And why do you have to be such a good sport about Hhy's pranks? You actually laughed at some of the things he did."

Red-faced with anger, Hymeron stepped closer to Alex. "Hhy's behaving like a wimp. I'm not surprised. Hhy's—." He stopped speaking and ground his teeth.

Alex shoved his face closer to Hymeron's. *This guy's such a jerk.* "Hhy's what?"

Hhy jabbed his brother in the ribs.

"Okay, I'm sorry," Hymeron said. "The worst of what happened was my fault."

Alex stared at the two of them. *It's so frustrating dealing with these two. They talk about things like this AI and never get around to explaining.* "Okay, but do you two remember Amable's threat of confining you to quarters? If you go back to doing stupid pranks, Amable will hear about it." *And regardless of how they behave, I'm going to make sure Amable hears about those other two aliens who tortured me in the hall. Wait, can I do that to Twarbie?* He remembered the alien girl pressed up against him and face tipped to his for a kiss. Then he remembered the sharp teeth and shuddered. *Ew, gross.*

"That's fair," Hhy said. He turned away from them and spoke over his shoulder. "Race you to the top of the hill."

"What hill?" Alex asked. Hhy laughed. Suddenly grass waved on the slope of a hill in front of them, and a warm breeze brought the smell of salt water to him. Warmth on his skin made him look up. Instead of a ceiling, a violet sky with puffy white clouds and two suns, one dull-red and the other yellow, met his eyes. His mouth dropped open. *This alien stuff could drive me crazy. I've got to roll with it.*

Alex ran up the hill after Hhy. "What happened? Where are we?"

Hymeron sprinted past Alex. "This is still the same room. Don't ask us how the Weird does this. We don't have a clue."

Alex struggled to keep up with Hymeron and finally collapsed on the ground, chest heaving.

~**********~

Vaguely, Alex knew he could wake-up. *It can't be morning. I want to sleep. I was having a good dream.*

Yesterday was such a hard day. It was better toward the end, but I'm so sore and tired, except... I don't really feel tired anymore. Experimentally he stretched. *I'm not even sore.* The idea of waking up seemed to be calling to him. He rolled over trying to reject the idea, but the desire to get up grew. With a half-hearted groan of disgust, he rolled back and blinked his eyes.

"Oh, you're awake."

"What?" Alex blinked again lifting his head from the pillow.

"The Weird said you didn't need to sleep anymore. It used a holo-field to hurry your recovery from yesterday. It said to get in here and get going with you. I've got some—"

"Whoa. Slow down," Alex said propping himself up.

Twarbie, kneeling next to him, leaned forward offering him a steaming bowl. "The Weird said this would help you get going, but the Weird has made it too hot. I don't know why it would do something so thoughtless. Let it cool or you'll burn yourself. It told me to try and help you wake-up, but I didn't think I was able to do it, but you woke-up."

Alex opened his mouth to speak, but Twarbie kept on talking. *Is she even taking a breath?*

"Did you feel the encouragement to get up? I—"

Alex pushed himself up at her and shouted, "You controlled me again?!"

He finished the shout even as he knocked the hot bowl of food over into her lap and hit her head with his knocking her over backward. The hot liquid soaked into her pantaloons and she screamed.

"Ow! Help!"

Sitting up she scooped the bowl and some of the thicker liquid away with her hands and then held her red hands in the air screaming and crying.

Alex reached forward with his hands. *What do I do? She needs her pantaloons off and something cold.* He reached forward going from thought to action, but stopped, embarrassment fumbling his thoughts. "Um, um, Weird, she needs her pantaloons off and something cold." In a moment of clarity, he added. "Just use a holo-field, but don't leave her naked." As he spoke he averted his gaze.

Her screams subsided and he risked a glance out of the corner of his eyes. Her legs were bare, but around her lap was an opaque pink cloud. Her hands had their own little pink clouds. He started to grin at the sight, but the rest of the view smashed the light heartedness of his response. Alex moved to her side at first unsure of what to do. Twarbie keened, a low wailing sound as she held both hands out from her body. Her head was tipped forward with her long hair sweeping back and forth. Awkwardly, he slipped an arm around her. "I'm sorry. I'm sorry. You're going to be okay."

The keening stopped and she pressed her face against him sobbing. Alex pulled her to him and whispered into her hair, "It's okay. You're going to be okay."

The Weird said, "She should be healed. The pain should be gone."

Still she sobbed. Lifting his head slightly, Alex noticed the pink cloud gone from her hands and the still bare legs. In a flat voice, he said, "Pantaloons, Weird."

The legs were covered and still she sobbed into his shirt as if she would never stop.

"Weird? Why's she still crying?"

"No idea. Talk to her."

Alex tried to think. *I'm holding an alien girl-teenager I'm guessing about my age, but I really have no clue at all. She controls me without thinking it's wrong. The pain of the hot food is long gone, and yet she's still crying. What can I say?* "Twarbie, I don't know what to say. I'm here for you and when you're ready we can talk."

With one hand, he gently smoothed her hair across her head. After what seemed like hours, her sobbing died away. Still, she didn't try to move away from him.

In a quiet voice she spoke, and he could feel her breath against him. "Now you know more about me. Getting burned terrifies me."

She paused, just breathing quietly against his chest. Alex tried to think of what to say. Twarbie continued speaking. Now Alex had to lean his head down closer to hear.

"My mom burns me every now and then. Once I thought she might've been crying while it happened, but I'm not sure because of my own screaming. Afterwards, she tells me I need to be tough and endure the pain. Her mother did it to her and if I have any kids, I'll need to learn how to do it to them. I can't. I don't want to. I won't. Then they'll kill me."

Aghast at the words, Alex pressed his head down against hers. "No. You won't have to. I'll help you." He thought of A'idah and her fiery spirit, of Zeghes and his adamant loyalty. "I know others who'll help you."

Twarbie shoved Alex away and he gazed in surprise at her.

Fear filled her voice. "No. Don't tell anyone else about me. I can't trust anyone."

What will she do? "Twarbie, what will you do when we leave here? Will you trust me when I leave?"

Twarbie stood to her feet. Her fisted hands turned white. "I don't know. You should know, I'm good at lying. I could lie, and say I'll always trust you with my life, but I don't want to, and I don't know. I just don't know."

The Weird said, "Twarbie, you'll need to leave before long."

She makes a real good story. Can I trust her? "Why did you use that control stuff to wake me up?"

"I didn't. The weird suggested I try using a vapuc called State of Mind."

Alex closed on her, jabbing a finger at her. "What's the difference? You were still controlling me."

"The reason winkles are good at the Controlling Animals vapuc is it works best when you don't care about what you're controlling. When I tried using it on you in the passageway it didn't work as good as it should. It was very strange, as if there were two sides to you. One I could see and liked and another I could control. The other vapuc, State of Mind, isn't controlling, but encouraging. It works best... when you...care... or.... . I didn't think it would work. Winkles aren't good at it." Changing her tone and speaking quickly, she said, "Amable is really good at 'State of Mind.' Some people think he can hypnotize, which would explain how he can talk people into doing what they don't want to."

81

The Weird interrupted, "Twarbie, you must leave, now."

Turning away from Alex, Twarbie sprinted for her door. "Bye."

"This is fine, just fine. She says all of that and then she has to leave. Now, what am I supposed to do? Just lie down and pretend to be a sleep again?"

"Yes."

Alex lay still with his thoughts rampaging. *Two sides to me. What did Gursha say about my illness? Could it be that? And what was Twarbie saying about care before she started rattling on about Amable?* Alex tried to jam his mind to a halt, as he waited for the kimleys.

Chapter Eleven
Training by Four Aliens

For weeks Alex spent long mornings with Twarbie. She started teaching him the movements of the winkle's form of martial arts. He remembered his initial confusion the first days of her training and how terribly the week had ended.

~**********~

"The winkle form of self-defense is cool, but when are you going to let me put more force into my kicks and hits? Are you afraid I'll hurt you?"

"What? We don't do defense. And you're not ready. You need to be stronger. Weird, help me out. Alex, stay there." That said, Twarbie moved away from Alex and sat down.

Alex shrugged. "Okay, now what?"

A tall thin manikin appeared. It reached a long arm out and slapped Alex. The next blows he blocked, but then another manikin appeared and slapped the back of his head. Getting slapped once startled and annoyed, but getting slapped multiple times blossomed those feelings into anger. Alex moved trying to get the two manikins where he could see and block both of them. In frustration, he snapped an angry question. "What am I supposed to do?"

"Figure it out."

The one to his left slapped the side of his head, while a new manikin slapped the back of his head. Alex squatted to avoid the blows and looked back. The manikin behind him swung a leg to kick him. *What?* Alex screamed in frustration. "Ahhhhh!" He kicked up and out. His foot connected with a satisfying crunch. The manikin blasted apart.

83

"Yeah!" Alex twisted about. He registered the blows of the other manikins, but ignored them. Standing up, he lashed out with another kick. That manikin shattered. Feeling cocky Alex bounced on his toes. "You want some of this?"

The last manikin swung his wooden hand in an attempt to slap. Alex lifted his arm catching the slap and redirecting it up and away. *I should follow the blow, twist my arm and grab its arm. Then I could pull it off balance and... I just want to kick it, hard.*

Alex lifted his right leg and swung it in an arc at the upper leg of the last slapper. *I like these shin kicks.* In another moment his shin bone connected and the wooden pieces of the manikin flew apart. "Yeah!"

One piece of wood came to rest under Alex. He stomped on it with his foot. Agony radiated up his leg. "I got your lesson. Ignore the pain and blast them."

Breathing hard, Alex looked around. Everything waited quiet and still. Twarbie sat with her hand over her eyes. *What? Why isn't she watching?* In the stillness, the sound of wood being crunched jerked his attention from her. Behind him another manikin advanced. Each step smashed pieces of wood under its big feet. Alex grinned. *The bigger they are, the harder they fall.* He started to bounce on his feet and stopped at the pain in one foot.

Without a sound, the manikin swung one arm slowly at Alex.

This is crazy. I could run around behind it before its hand reaches me. Alex stepped back and watched as the manikin slowly followed through with the slap. *This is going to be even easier. I could just push it over, but I like kicking them to pieces.* Wincing a little at the pain in his foot, Alex took the time to position himself right for another shin kick. *Ha. This one's moving so slowly.* Almost laughing-out-loud at the ease of his victory, Alex began his kick. Thoughts flashed through his mind. *Rotate the foot I'm standing on. This turns my hips and makes for a stronger attack.* There was something else about turning-opening the hips Alex couldn't remember. The pain in the foot he stood on persuaded him to not rotate the foot. *No problem. I'll just swing my leg faster and harder. I'll show Twarbie how hard I can hit. She'll be impressed.*

Alex drove his leg forward. The manikin lifted a leg surprisingly fast to block the kick. *No problem, I'll just blast on through it.*

A sickening crunch, similar to the sound of a stick breaking, but wetter like a stalk of celery being broken filled the air. The manikin only wobbled a little. *What happened?* Sudden pain blasted his mind. Alex hobbled backward. He could see a new bend below his knee. The lower part of his leg hung like a limp noodle.

For a long moment, he stared in shock as he slipped to the ground. A blue-pink haze appeared around his leg. The last thing Alex noticed was the leg, his leg, straightening out.

Eyes closed, Alex heard a voice.

"You idiotic boy.... Why couldn't you listen to me?"

Alex gasped. *My leg?* The pain was gone. Blinking he opened his eyes, slowly focusing on Twarbie's pink shoes. Tipping his head back he looked up at her face. Tears coursed down her cheeks as she spoke.

"Pain is a sure way of helping the memory. You haven't been paying attention. Before you can hit harder, you must get your bones stronger. Technique always has to be perfect. I wouldn't have agreed with the Weird in doing this, except for what it tells me. The Weird thinks you knowing the winkle martial arts might keep you alive during this year. You have to learn and remember what I teach you."

After that horrible day, her lessons and techniques stuck much better in his mind. Two he remembered in particular. The first he figured out on his own and never told Twarbie. She did surprise attacks on him, and he learned to recognize the sound her feet made, as she started an attack. The other was a lecture he got as a result of a question. He'd asked, "What's the most important element of the winkle form of self-defense?"

"I already told you this isn't self-defense. Learning to just defend is stupid. If your mindset is to defend yourself, then you're more than halfway to defeat. Ideally you walk looking not for what to defend against, but what to attack or as some other species put it, predators attack and prey defend. Eventually, predators will always eat the prey."

She snorted and continued. "There's something else you need to remember, and don't make me to teach it to you the painful way. Don't always advance on your opponent. Sometimes attack by retreating is the only option."

~**********~

The first time Alex beat the kimleys at a race, an out-of-breath Hhy said, "Now that baby lepercaul... would never catch you."

The comment stuck in his head, along with questions. What ever happened to the lepercaul? Did Twarbie even worry about it? She says she wants to be different, but it looks like she left the baby to fend for itself.

The next morning he asked Twarbie. "Why did you abandon the baby lepercaul?"

Twarbie looked down at the ground. "Um, after meeting you.... I kinda lost track of time. I'd never met anyone like you.

"After Hymeron contacted me about the baby chasing you, I tried to come to your aid. Once I got to where Hymeron told me to find the portal, it had disappeared. I think the zorms closed it. For a moment, I didn't know what to do. I didn't know how to make a new one, so I contacted Hymeron. He said, 'Not to worry about it. He had an idea for an escape.' I wasn't happy leaving the baby with the zorms. Finally, I came to the Weird to make sure you were okay. When I entered the door, I found myself in an empty room, which surprised me. The ship had told me you were in the Weird.

"Then, the Weird started talking to me. It suggested the idea of my staying in a secret room for the months of your training."

With a big grin, she said, "I jumped at the opportunity to get a break from my life out in the real world."

"Oh," Alex said. *What do I say? Doesn't she feel responsible for the baby?*

As if she heard his thought, Twarbie said, "After our first meeting in the Weird, I began to worry about the baby. I contacted the ship, and it told me the zorms had salted the lepercaul."

"Salted it?" A vision of a dead baby lepercaul lying in salt popped into Alex's mind. "What does that mean?"

"They sprinkled it with salt, which causes a baby lepercaul to start changing into the adult form. They sweat a liquid and shrink in size. Also, it causes them to lose the ability to feed just by touching something."

"Why would they do that?"

"I'm not sure. The ship wouldn't tell me."

Alex remembered the secret crystal forest. *I'm glad I didn't break any of the crystals. The baby had probably broken some crystal, but how would salting the baby help?* "So, it's no longer dangerous?"

"For now it isn't. Eventually as lepercauls get older they grow very strong at using force. Then they are even more dangerous than the babies."

"Wow. How can you fight someone who's that dangerous?"

"With your AI, if you are really good at using gravity generators. If you can keep from getting hurt or killed, eventually the lepercaul or anyone doing vapuc will get tired. And back to the baby just starting to become an adult, new adults will get tired quite quickly."

She paused and Alex stood quietly for a moment considering what Twarbie had said. She continued. "There are things called enhancers, which can increase one's abilities with vapuc. They're quite dangerous for the user, but it would let someone dominate everyone else for a short period of time."

Alex thought of another question. "How did you get the baby from the wild?"

"Easy. Winkles keep a stockpile of salt near the lepercaul's wild area. The ship has storage chambers all over the place. All you have to do is stand to the right of the wild doorway, and ask the ship to open the salt chamber. I took some salt in a small bag, stepped into the wild, and waited for a good sized baby to come along. Then, I threatened it with the salt. They know salt hurts. After I told it the plan, it came along quite willingly. One thing I goofed on. I should've gotten it from the other side of the wild. I didn't want to attempt going all the way through the wild with just salt for defense, so I went the long way around. Going through passageways, I didn't pay attention to the baby and it got away. I asked the ship for help, but sometimes the ship isn't real helpful. That was one of those times. I was lucky I had gotten the baby a day early to practice with it."

Alex took away a number of things from the talk. Twarbie really did seem to have at least a part of her which considered others. Unless of course she lied, but he wanted to believe her. The salt stuff was interesting, but no way would he ever use salt to try and control a baby lepercaul.

~**********~

One evening the two suns had set, and clusters of bright stars started appearing in the sky.

"Wow, what a sunset or was it a suns-set?" Alex asked, smiling at the boys, while they all sat around a fire enjoying dinner. The last few days had been fun, especially this day when he dunked them in the pool. *Why did Hhy insist on wearing a vest in the water? Hymeron just wore shorts.*

Hhy quietly said, "This is the view from our home planet."

"Hhy, I bet you love it there," Alex said. When the kimley didn't respond, Alex looked at him. "What's wrong?"

Hhy frowned. "You aren't pronouncing my name right. It's Hhy, not Hi."

"I'm sorry, Hhhhy." Alex said, trying to get the aspirated h sound right. Something about Hhy drew him toward the boy. Alex reached toward him. "Why the sad face?"

Sighing, Hhy said, "We've never been to our home world. No kimley lives there anymore. I wish we weren't reminded of it."

"What happened?"

"Our people were attacked... and sold into slavery."

"That's terrible."

Hhy shrugged. "It isn't as bad now. Some of us have been freed."

Then the stars were gone, and three game controllers appeared next to Hhy. With a forced grin, he reached for one of them. "Now for some games."

"Wait. If your home world makes you sad, why did you have the Weird make it seem like we were on your home world?"

Hymeron scowled. "We didn't. The Weird decides the scenes. We can ask for things and make suggestions, but it's in control."

Surprised, Alex looked at Hhy. He nodded in agreement. Alex said, "But, aren't you boys controlling my training?"

Hhy stood up. "We're just two kids good at playing pranks and games. The Weird doesn't need us for your training. Right now, it looks like we should play some games."

"No, the Weird can wait," Alex said.

The ground shook and a rumble filled the air. Hhy held a game controller out to Alex. "The Weird doesn't like to wait."

"Tough. I want to understand more about your past."

Hhy dropped back to the ground and sat, head bowed, and white hair cascading over his face. Hymeron moved close to him and put an arm around him. "There isn't much to understand. We don't have any home world. Everyone uses or enslaves us. People kill us all the time, and there are fewer and fewer of us left."

Leaning forward Alex placed a hand on Hhy's shoulder. "That's terrible. Why are your people treated this way?"

Hymeron's mouth formed a straight angry line across his face. "You think *that's* terrible. Listen to this. It all started when other people in the galaxy found out about us. Our parents' conscious awareness lives in the future. That means they know some of the future possibilities. An adult kimley risks his health and life whenever he shares that knowledge with another individual. The more it affects the course of the present, the more likely the adult will die if he shares it. Others don't care about our lives. A few years ago, one individual killed thousands of kimleys trying to learn more about the role of your planet in the future."

"Who?" Alex asked.

Hhy jerked his head up to glare at Alex, and he spat the name. "Maleky."

"Most people are afraid to even say his name," Hymeron said. "Not us, we hate him. He kidnapped one of our cousins."

Alex felt overwhelmed by the information and not sure what to say. "At least you're safe."

Hhy gave a short, bitter laugh. "Our cousin was at the Academy when he was kidnapped, but we're not afraid."

Hymeron nodded. "He was almost as old as my sister, Hheilea, is now. That's the age we're in the most danger."

"I didn't know you two have a sister," Alex said.

Hhy shrugged. "It doesn't matter. Someone will probably kidnap her or if she's lucky, kill her in the attempt. No one cares enough to save m—, her."

Alex reached out to pull both boys into a hug. "You said others don't care about your lives. Reconsider that statement. I care." Confused thoughts and feelings flowed through him. *These kids behaved terrible, well mostly Hymeron, but it sounds as if life is horrible for them.*

Hhy held his arms crossed in front of him, as Alex hugged the two of them.

"Let's do the video games tomorrow evening," Hymeron said.

Alex said, "Good idea, Hymeron. Do you know the names of those spiral galaxies hanging above us?"

The night sky had reappeared above them. After the star gazing, Alex found the Weird had him lying in a hammock. In the warm air his shorts were just right. Next to him Hhy and Hymeron each lay in separate hammocks, which were suspended from tree trunks. High above them, feathery fronds moved against the starry sky. In the background, he could hear the lapping of waves.

Opening his eyes the next morning, Alex watched the fronds of the two palm-like trees rustling. The warm breeze blew gently over his bare chest. Now he understood why they got into so much trouble. *They have fortune tellers for parents. Maybe they would tell him about his future. Wait, that's not a good idea. That would hurt their parents. Couldn't they tell me just a little? Where did that thought come from.* His Mom and Dad would never want him to hurt others for his own gain. *What's wrong with me?* Another thought, one he happily latched onto as safer slipped into his mind. *Hheilea, that's a pretty name. I wonder why I haven't heard about her before.*

At the sound of splashing, Alex lifted his head. Someone was swimming toward him. *Twarbie?* He twisted about trying to get out of the hammock, but moved too quickly and found himself flipped onto the sand. Alex got up on his hands and knees. *Twarbie shouldn't be here. The kimleys could see her. I should... We....*

Even as he tried to think he watched Twarbie wading out of the water. She had on an emerald green bikini and the view swallowed up his thoughts. "Uh... The... kimleys."

Twarbie said, "The Weird's keeping them asleep."

Tipping his head back, he continued to watch as she walked up onto the sand. *Oh my.... Wow.... She's.... Stay cool. I can deal with this. Just act like the unflustered British spy.*

"Are you going to stay on your knees?"

"Oh." Alex jumped to his feet, brushing against her in the motion. His face flamed. "S— Sorry."

He stumbled back, just stopping as the hammock hit the back of his legs. *I'm acting like a fool. Wait! She knows this.* He remembered her words. *'Also, I was taught how to appeal to males, to make them easier to control.' She's an alien and still trying to control me.* He took a step forward and anger flooded his voice. "Weird, put some clothes on her."

Nothing happened.

"The Weird told me to swim to you in this bikini. I didn't choose this..., but I have to admit your reaction was fun, until you got mad."

"Weird, what are you doing?" *She's an alien with sharp pointed teeth. I bet they file their teeth. It's stupid to be attracted to her.*

She ruefully grinned at him. "It talks to me when you're gone. The Weird's interesting. I wouldn't try to guess what it's up to."

The Weird wouldn't be trying to... Her teeth aren't pointed anymore. "Your teeth."

"The Weird helped me get them back to normal. I thought you would find me easier to be with." Twarbie took a step closer. "What do you think?"

She grinned. Her teeth were normal, not pointed or sharp looking.

"Uh, yeah."

Her grin fell away to a frown. "Ugh, guys. Is your brain turned off by my bikini?"

Alex's gaze started to travel back down, but he forced it back to her eyes. They weren't much better. He could drown in them. "No.... Well... a bit, but you already know how you can affect a guy."

She went from a frown to a pout. "Yes. And it's frustrating with you. I'm trying to change. I hoped you'd like the new me, but I'm beginning to think you can't see past the shape of my flesh."

Finishing her complaint Twarbie pivoted on one foot and flounced back toward the water.

Alex followed. *She's right. I don't have a clue about these aliens, especially the girls, by just looking at them.* The fact *she's so attractive doesn't help.*

Right at the edge of the water, Twarbie whirled about and as she did everything changed. The bikini disappeared. The blonde-red-brunette locks were gone. Instead of a teenage winkle girl, a black figure with big scaly wings and claws for hands faced Alex.

For a second he froze trying to comprehend what just happened. The creature opened a cavernous mouth revealing long dripping fangs. Alex stumbled back a step. *It's just the Weird doing something strange.* Tentatively he asked, "Twarbie?"

The beast in front of him bellowed, it almost sounded like laughter. "Ha, I beat the Weird. It thought you would stumble backward, get tangled up in your hammock, and fall into the sand."

"What has the Weird done? You look like some horrible beast."

The beast-Twarbie spread wings about twenty feet from wing tip to wing tip. "What do you think of my new look?"

"It's a thing of nightmares." Red eyes blazed from a face dominated by a maw big enough to hold a small melon.

"This is the type of deem called a gaahr. They normally grow to about seven to eight-feet tall and with a wing span of about thirty feet. Check out my tail."

Alex stepped forward and ran a hand along the leathery tail which curled from behind her.

"Careful of the barb at the end of the tail, it's really sharp."

He pulled his hand back from the three-inch-long claw like barb on the end of the tail. The gaahr-Twarbie stood dressed in only dark-red and gold leather straps. Alex stared at the creature. Some areas of it were blurred as if out of focus. The rest was covered with bristly black hair. "Why can't I see part of you?"

"Deems are composed of normal matter and Dark Matter. Different types of Dark Matter do strange things to light. What do you think of my jewels?"

A necklace hung from the beast's neck and more jewels studded the leather straps on her torso.

"They look strange on a beastly creature like this."

"Never, ever forget deems are not just beasts. Most of them are highly intelligent. Remember, they built this ship."

"Oh. Yeah." Alex reached to check out the leather straps running across her body.

"Hey, watch where you're putting your hands. It's still me here."

The image flashed through Alex's mind of where his hand would've been on Twarbie and he backed up against one of the tree trunks. "Sorry. Wasn't thinking."

"It's—"

The ground started shaking sending Twarbie staggering about.

Alex braced himself with one arm around the trunk and called to her. "Come here. The trunk's stable."

She staggered to him and with a scrunching sound dug the claws of one hand into the tree.

He slipped his other arm around Twarbie to help steady her. *This is silly. In her beast form she's stronger than me.* Another thought, one not so readily accepted by him, crossed his mind. *She's probably stronger than me in her normal form.*

The shaking stopped as quickly as it started. The beast was gone. Alex had his arm around the warm back of Twarbie. He let go of the tree trunk and looked down into her eyes.

Twarbie grinned and hugged him to her. Excitedly she chattered away. "You did great with that exercise. The Weird wants you to learn about looking past what the outward looks like."

Her voice slowed down as Alex held her to him. Ignoring the alarms going off in his mind and heart he slowly began moving a hand on her smooth back.

"It... it's going to be important... in the future for you to... think about deems as intelligent people... not as beasts."

"I'm not thinking about you as Twarbie, the terrible winkle. I think you're honestly changing."

"Thanks." Quickly she said, "I should go. Weird? Isn't it time for me to go?"

"I don't hear it answering." *Tropical beach and a girl I like. This is good. Except...*

Twarbie placed her hands against Alex's chest and gently pushed. "Please, let me go."

With a sigh, he released her. Twarbie backed up. Alex gazed into her eyes and began to follow, but she placed a hand against him and pushed. "No."

Alex backed up and Twarbie disappeared. Even her foot prints on the sand were gone. He continued to back up as he thought about the girl. *She might be an alien, but I like her. I'm crazy. I don't need this. I wish she hadn't left.* He felt the hammock hit the back of his legs, but didn't care and didn't think as he backed up more. Taking one too many steps backward, he lost his balance landing back first into the hammock. It flipped sending him face first into the sand. He lifted his head to spit out the sand in his mouth and then rested his head back down. *I think I'll just stay here.*

Chapter Twelve
Hheilea

The sand was no longer under him. He rested in the hammock. *What?* Suddenly, Hhy lay beside him, and Alex had an arm around him. Music in his head soared. Alex pulled his arm back in embarrassment as Hhy rolled out of the hammock. Hhy's quick exit swung the hammock, dumping Alex and Hymeron, who had also been deposited into the hammock, onto the sand below.

Untangling himself from a struggling Hymeron and after spitting out sand again, Alex asked, "What happened?"

Hhy said, "For some strange reason the Weird put me in your hammock, and I jumped out."

Alex shrugged. *That was strange. Why did the Weird do that? And why have my arm around Hhy? Did I hear music?* "What? Why did you jump out?" Alex helped Hymeron to his feet. "Hhy, you're all red. Are you embarrassed? Why—? Oh, well I guess I don't know what's embarrassing for your people."

Hhy said, with a strained voice. "I'm sorry. Being dumped into your hammock startled me."

Alex brushed himself off and awkwardly laughed. "Oh well, no harm done." *What's the Weird up too? This is too much. Throwing Twarbie at me in a bikini. Okay, I did enjoy that. Even if I'm really rattled by her, but having my arm around Hhy in a hammock.* An uncomfortable silence grew around him. *What's safe to talk about?* Alex asked, "Hhy? Something has been bothering me since last night. How come I haven't heard before about your sister, Hheilea?"

Hymeron and Hhy looked at each other. They both turned to Alex and spoke at the same time.

Hhy said, "She isn't on the ship."

Hymeron said, "She stays hidden in our rooms with Mom."

Alex said, slowly puzzling things out, "Aren't your rooms on this ship?"

Again both kimleys answered at once.

Hymeron said, "I meant our rooms back at the Academy."

Hhy said, "We aren't supposed to tell people she's on the ship."

Alex crossed his arms, frowning. "You two are hiding something."

Again, the two kimleys looked at each other. Hymeron shrugged, and Hhy turned to Alex. "I'm sorry, but for her safety we don't talk about her."

In a rush and sounding a little desperate, Hymeron said, "Today we teach you how to play videogames, and Alex, you're so going to get beat."

Alex said. "Ha. You should know videogames are a teenage boy's favorite pastime on my world. You might not beat me as easily as you expect." In a more serious tone, he continued. "I'm okay if you don't trust me with information about your sister, but please, don't lie. Everything's so strange. I don't know who to trust."

Hhy hesitantly came up to Alex and gave him a hug. "I'm sorry, Alex. I do want to trust you."

Hymeron spoke up louder than normal. "If you're good at videogames, the Weird will just make it harder so much sooner."

Alex pushed Hhy away forcing him to break the hug. *That was awkward.* He cleared his throat. "Okay, Hymeron. Let's get started."

~**********~

Many nights later, Alex tossed and turned trying to sleep. Finally, he rolled to his back and stared up at a black sky. "Why don't you use the holo-fields to put me to sleep? Then I'll be rested to give Twarbie some time."

"I considered it, but I thought you needed time to think."

"You thought, huh? All of this is just...." *I want to scream.*

"If it helps, I think you're doing a great job of pretending with the kimleys. I don't know much about humans, but if they're all like you, I think Earth might have a chance."

I'm doing great, he says. It's obvious the Weird can't read minds. I think I'm going crazy. The events and emotions with Twarbie are spiraling out of my control. As if I was ever in control. And if that isn't enough, I think Hhy is acting really strange. If he was a human I'd think he's attracted to me. I don't want a guy attracted to me in that way. At least Twarbie's a girl, even if she is still an alien. Then there's my fear I'm attracted to Hhy. I can't look at him without feeling something is drawing me closer. I've got to hold it together until I get out of here. I'll be back with the other Earthlings and everything will be normal. Yeah, talking animals and a family group composed of me, a dolphin, and a Kalasha girl. "Please just put me to sleep."

Alex drifted off to sleep with one last thought. *At least things can't get worse. Just got to hold it together, until I can get back to the flock.*

The desire to wake-up crept into his dreams. Gently it pulled him to awareness. *She's here.* Alex sat up and waited for the hammock to stop moving. As he swung his legs over the side, he looked around at the tropical vegetation trying to spot Twarbie. For weeks now, this was their morning ritual. The Weird kept the kimleys asleep. Twarbie would gently wake him up, and he would try and find her. A table top sized leaf moved slightly, and Alex spotted the blonde-red-brunette mix of her hair. He looked carefully at the terrain between them. Too many times he'd been caught, jerked, and held upside down by a skillfully hidden trap. A thick branch's leaves were at a different angle from the rest of the plant's leaves. He recognized the bend to the branch and a taut vine running down from it toward the ground. He grinned at the obvious alternative. Yesterday, he'd tried to avoid a trap to get to her and had fallen into a hidden pit full of water. *She won't get me that way today.* The path from him to her led right through the trap location. To the right of the path was a smooth area. After a quick glance under the edge of the hammock showed it to be safe, he pushed off and stood, bending he reached for the stick he'd hidden. *I'll just use my stick and set off her trap with—* His thoughts were interrupted by a snapping sound and a tug on his arm. "Ah!"

In a second he found himself dragged across the ground and into a big pool of soupy cold mud. Laughter bubbled out of Twarbie's hiding spot.

Standing up, Alex waded through the mud. "Please, remove the cord and the mud from my face."

Twarbie stepped from under the huge leaf. "Uh, why didn't you get rid of all the mud?"

Nonchalantly Alex kept moving closer to her. "Didn't you know? Mud is good for the skin. It feels good."

He raised both muddy hands at her. Twarbie gave a squeal and turned to run, with Alex right behind her. In a few strides she tripped over a hidden cord and tumbled into the undergrowth. In a second Alex caught her and gave her a big muddy hug. After thoroughly rubbing his muddy hands over her face and hair he released her and stood. "Thanks for your help, Weird, in setting this up. Now how about clean clothes and no mud."

The two of them stood grinning at each other. Twarbie said, "Breakfast, please." A table loaded with food and two chairs appeared."

As Alex took his last bite and leaned back with a sigh, he realized Twarbie was just sitting looking at him. "What?"

"I want us to stay here forever."

Alarms went off in Alex's head. "Hey. Remember we're just going to be friends?" *But that isn't what I want.*

The previous day she'd been working with him on his efforts to learn the winkle form of martial arts. For the twentieth or thirtieth time Alex had been flipped to the ground. The last time instead of offering him a hand up, she'd dropped to her knees beside him. Fumbling at first and then in a rush, she'd asked, "Is it.... Could I.... Can I kiss you?"

Alex could feel his face growing warm at the memory. He'd said, "Remember? We said we'd try to be friends. Kissing isn't being friends." The worst of it was he'd wanted the kiss in the worst way. *But she's an alien. Fortunately, the Weird had Twarbie leave.*

Twarbie shoved her unfinished plate of food. It slid off the table and disappeared. Eyes pinning Alex to his chair, she leaned across the table, grasped Alex's plate and flipped it away. *What's she doing?* He couldn't bring himself to say anything or move. She said, surprising him with her matter of fact tone, "I've never had a friend before, except once I almost did. When we leave here you shouldn't be my friend, but I thought some friends kiss. Stick and Gursha seem to be great friends and they definitely kiss." What Twarbie said next was filled with emotion. "I want you to kiss me, please."

Emotionally, she's like a little kid-teenager-refugee or something, but right now who am I to speak. My own emotions are a mess. "You're right about friends being able— Wait, you said I shouldn't be your friend when we leave here? Why?"

Twarbie backed up and sat down. The table between them disappeared and Alex followed her gaze. She twisted her hands and rubbed them together in her lap. Glancing back up, Alex caught a quick look from her. Twarbie ducked her head again. Hesitantly she started to talk, and the more she said the more subdued her voice became. "Years ago, Amable tried to force the winkles to integrate with the others he's brought together. For a short time, I went to a school with non-winkles and was taught by a non-winkle. One classmate had metal hair and could make sparks. I had fun with her. Then she died. My mother, the powerful Dweistickle, had told me not to be friendly. The winkle mutiny happened right after that. I remember having to watch as a winkle was forced to torture a friend she'd made. It took all day for the friend to die, and then the winkle was killed...." Twarbie jumped to her feet and her voice jumped too, full of pain and defeat. "I should leave. Just forget about me."

Alex leapt out of his chair and.... *I'm an idiot. This is crazy.* Pushing through the screams of logic and fear he rushed to close the distance as the huge-amazing-alien eyes of hers locked into his and grew even larger as his intent became apparent. Alex grasped both of her slim shoulders in his hands and pulled her to him. Their lips met. A sweetness filled his mouth and he staggered, releasing her and almost stumbling, he gasped. Her hands caught him just before he fell and held him close. In awe, she asked, "Why did you kiss me?"

"You wanted it, I wanted it. What happened? It was incredible."

"Our kisses are intoxicating to many male species. We.... I.... Oh, Alex, there's so much you haven't learned about me. I shouldn't have come into the Weird, but I can't imagine not staying. Please forgive me."

Breathing deep, Alex relished the feelings of Twarbie and her arms about him. "Don't be afraid to live life. Someone once told me, if you live life well you're going to lose people, but if you never lived then you never had them to lose."

Gently the Weird said, "Twarbie, Twarbie, you need to go."

She clutched at Alex's back and crushed him to her, and then pushed him away. "That was wonderful, you're wonderful, but I'm so scared. Forget about this. Good bye."

Twarbie walked away and disappeared. For a long moment, Alex looked off in the direction she must be and then he returned to his hammock. Once again, he pretended to sleep, waiting for his day with the kimleys to start.

The next few days, Alex and the kimleys did exercise activities during the day, followed by videogames in the evening. Not wanting to think about how things were going with Twarbie, Alex immersed himself in the training. *I wish I was too tired for the Weird to have me working with her*. He just couldn't handle the pain. In the last sessions, Twarbie had broken many of his bones with the fierceness of her training. He remembered yesterday.

~**********~

They stood on a flat plain surrounded by low hills. Twarbie jabbed at his face, and Alex barely deflected the blow. Compared to her, he felt so slow. She stomped on his foot and pain lanced up his leg. Alex stumbled backward. "I think you broke my foot."

"This lesson is about pain. Ignore it."

Alex fought to stand normaly, balanced and ready to—. Dancing around him, Twarbie snapped quick punishing blows. "Move faster."

He tried to move faster, but his arms moved too slow. In frustration, he yelled at her. "Stop!"

Surprisingly, she did. Twarbie stood in front of him, chest heaving, and face red. She yelled back. "Too much for you?! You just don't get it!"

"Yes. This is too much pain. How are you moving so fast?"

"This is a taste of what it would be like if—"

The Weird interrupted. "Twarbie, I too am having trouble with this scene you wanted."

Gratefully Alex said, "Thanks. Can you heal me?"

"No!" Twarbie attacked. "Weird show him."

Alex gritted his teeth against the pain and frustration. It wasn't fair. He couldn't move fast enough. Around them materialized rows and rows of robed figures. A chant filled the air. Evil pressed against Alex, and he fought just to breathe. Twarbie grabbed his arm and twisted it back behind him. Pain ripped through his shoulder. She let go of his arm. "How does that feel?"

He couldn't move his arm. The pain in his shoulder didn't go away. Some of the winkles surrounding them flickered in and out of view. The Weird said, "I'm going to need to close this scenario."

"You can't. Alex has to understand. This is what the other winkles will force me to do and much worse. You will slowly get beaten to a broken bloody pulp by me, by me." She struck Alex in the face and he could feel bones breaking, but he couldn't fight back or even try to move.

He could still see. In front of him Twarbie stood still, tears running down her face. In the background, the winkles vanished. "You have to understand. I can't stand the thought of killing you. You have to fear what the winkles can do. I can't care for you. We can't be friends. They'll find out. They always do. And then I'll be forced to kill you."

She hit him again in the face, and he started to choke on his own blood. He dropped falling onto his back. Vaguely he heard Twarbie screaming at the Weird. "He's dying! Heal him!"

"I can't. My processes are d—. I told you, whenever I — simulate that kind of evil it be— affect me. K— him a–ive"

Alex felt Twarbie roll him over onto his side. She pleaded. "Don't die." Fingers probed in his mouth. "Please, don't die."

He gasped for air. His view shifted pink and the physical pain ebbed.

With a ragged voice, Twarbie said, "This is how my mother would've taught me. I hate her teachings, but I'm her. I don't know how to be different. Somehow, I have to keep you safe."

~**********~

Alex wanted to have confidence in her ability to change, but he just didn't know. The physical danger didn't discourage him like she wanted, instead he found her more attractive than ever. He tried talking with her about the future, but she refused. Even though he had the answer, he kept asking himself. *Why's she pushing me away?* Alex refused the thought which came in response, but he knew. *She's afraid. I should be afraid too. What's happening to me? Am I falling in love with an alien?* It no longer seemed so gross. One thing he understood, thinking about Twarbie hurt, and here he was doing it again. *I've got to stop thinking about her.*

One evening, Hymeron said, "You're doing great. I'm looking forward to tomorrow. We get to be in the game."

"What do you mean 'in the game'?" Alex asked. *Just this morning, Twarbie told me to get my head in the game. And tomorrow I'll have to see her again.*

"It'll be easier to show you," Hhy said.

The next day, the kimleys wore shorts and running shoes, with their white hair tied back in ponytails. Hymeron had ditched his shirt and vest, but Hhy still had on a tight vest. In his hands, he held a semi-translucent mass. "This is your new type of controller. It's a computer and much—."

Alex held up a hand and walked up to Hhy. *Something's going on, and I'm going to get some answers.* "Wait. I've wanted to ask why you're so different. Do kimley boys change as they get older?"

Hhy's voice squeaked, as he answered the question with a question. "What do you mean?"

Hymeron tried to interrupt. "We need to get going."

Alex moved closer to Hhy. "Your voice is higher than Hymeron's, your legs are very slender compared to his, and your hips are wider. And your face is shaped much different. Like how I think an elven—."

Hymeron shoved between them. "Come on, we have to explain your new controller. Stop being goofy. Of course everyone is different."

Alex held his hands up in surrender. *Someday Hymeron you're going to go too far. I'm just trying to understand what's going on around me.* "Okay. How do I use this?"

Hhy said, "Kneel in front of me."

With a shrug, Alex obeyed. *And now I'm supposed to ask you to marry me. Eck! Mentally he wanted to spit that thought and the memory out of his mind. Where did that come from? I so don't want to be stuck with these aliens any longer.* Even distracted by his crazy thoughts he could feel the surprisingly warm mass settling onto his scalp.

Hhy said, "It's your personal, artificial intelligence, AI for short. Stand up and look at my scalp. Both Hymeron and I have one too. It interfaces with your brain. With your AI, you'll be able to communicate with other people and access other computers. Eventually, it'll develop its own personality."

As Hhy spoke, Alex looked up into his eyes and for some reason remembered looking into Twarbie's eyes back in the passageway with his lips puckered up. Frantic thoughts blasted through his mind. *What's going on? Hhy isn't a girl and he's another alien.*

Hhy looked down at the ground. "This AI will always be with you. Physically, I think you're doing great. Now, we're going to help you learn things to survive out in the real world."

Hymeron impatiently said, "Let's get started. He'll catch on."

Suddenly Alex found himself with the boys on an eight-foot by eight-foot platform of grass. In front of it, other platforms, some short and some long, floated in the air. To the right and to the left, stone walls stretched out of sight. Alex moved to the edge of the platform and looked under it. Quickly, he backed up. "This platform's floating."

Hymeron shrugged. "Sort of. It's like the first videogame we played, except now you're inside the game. The goal is to find the coins and exit to the next level without dying. After you finish this game, we're doing one where we can fight with swords. I'm looking forward to it."

"Without dying?" Alex asked, his voice squeaking. "I thought the Weird wouldn't kill anyone."

"You don't physically die," Hhy said. "You won't feel pain if you miss a jump or get caught in a trap, like that one." Hhy pointed toward a set of tall sharp stakes standing in a pit. "You just lose a game life, and find yourself on a grass platform like this at the beginning of the level. If you lose too many lives, the game is over and you lose. I hope you beat this game quickly."

Hymeron jumped to another platform, a wooden one, and Alex followed. *I wish I could talk to the Weird. I bet it could move these platforms for me, but that would give away the time I've been spending with Twarbie. I'll just have to keep pretending I don't know how to get the Weird to do things.* A little later, Alex jumped at a moving grass platform, and missing it let out a yell as he fell. Below him were sharp stakes, their points glittered, and with his heart in his mouth he fell. For a second, he started to yell to the Weird for help, but stopped himself. A strange sensation made him scrunch up his shoulders, and then he stood gasping on the original platform feeling very glad there wasn't any pain.

This time when he came to the moving platform, he timed his jump and made it. Ahead, he watched Hhy drop off a platform falling straight down past a whole column of coins. The coins disappeared with a chiming sound. *This game is just like a normal videogame.* Back on Earth it would've been amazing to play a game this way, but he wanted to get to the sword fighting as quickly as possible.

Alex ignored the coins and watched how Hymeron traversed each level. He had to holler 'wait up' a couple of times, but he finally remembered the rhythm from the regular game. In front of him, he saw Hymeron watch swinging logs as he waited for the perfect timing to jump past them. When it was Alex's turn, he made the jump with ease. With one last leap he joined the two kids on the last platform, and then they stood on a grassy hill. Above them, fireworks shot off. A victory song started playing.

Alex asked, "Now do we get to use swords?"

"You did a great job of using your AI," Hhy said.

"What? I didn't need it."

"There's another game we could do. It would force you to use your AI more," Hymeron said with a grin.

Alex frowned. "You said we would do the sword fighting next." A thought occurred to him. "I want to do the sword fighting, but you said I would be learning things to help me survive in the real world. How will sword fighting help in the real world?" *Twarbie's teaching me the winkle's form of martial arts and how to resist the 'Controlling Animals' vapuc. But sword fighting?*

Hymeron sat down. "The most dangerous threat in the universe is deems. Their technology is the best anyone has. The most advanced weapons of your world will be useless. But deems love physical fights, and swords work great for fighting them, and for some deems very special swords work the best."

"That's good to know," Alex said. *I better remember. The other Earthlings need to know this.* "I remember Ytell talking about deems. They sound terrible."

Hymeron said, "They are. Did Ytell make clear they aren't just beasts, but are actually very intelligent with a higher level of technology than other civilizations?"

"I think so," Alex said, and then he paused. *I want to get back, but to what? My friends or back to Twarbie.* Alex took a long couple of deep breaths. *I feel like I'm drowning with her. She's climbing out of the water which is probably good because she's an alien and very dangerous to have even as a friend. I'm afraid I'm thinking of her more than as a friend.* "It's been a long time since I saw my friends in the flock. I want to get back. How fast can I do this sword training?"

As soon as Alex spoke his surroundings changed. A stone wall appeared next to him. A scabbard with a sword hung from a belt about his waist. He heard a single word, filled with pathos, echo down from above. "No!"

Backing away from the wall he looked up. Behind the wall, he could see the top of a tower. He paused as wind chimes sounded in his mind. *What's going on?* For the first time, he really heard the sounds. *Is that music in my head?* A slim woman in a white dress, with a loose yellow and green vest stood on top of the tower, her white hair waving in the wind.

From beside Alex, Hymeron yelled, "Weird! What are you doing?"

Alex quickly glanced down at Hymeron and back up to stare at the young woman. *Where was Hhy? That voice.*

Again, from above came the tragic word. "No!"

Alex recognized the voice. It all clicked. Hhy's voice was higher than Hymeron's. They were keeping a secret about a sister. Danger lurked for the sister. Hhy was the secret sister. Alex pointed up at the woman and said to Hymeron, "Hhy and your sister, Hheilea, are the same person."

Chapter Thirteen
Sword Fighting

Hymeron clutched his hair with both hands. "Yes. I don't know what the Weird's doing. It shouldn't have known about my sister. We've got to get her down. She needs to stay in her disguise."

Whenever Alex looked at Hheilea he was certain music sounded in his head and the song seemed familiar. *Didn't I hear it before.* Just then an arrow shot into the ground at Alex's feet. He jumped back. "Someone's shooting at me. Why am I hearing music? And why do we need to get her down?"

"Hurry, hurry," Hymeron said, sounding desperate. "The Weird's starting this scene."

Another arrow struck near Alex's feet. He dodged to the side. A bit panicked by the scene and arrows, he asked, "Where are these arrows coming from? What am I supposed to do?"

Hymeron said, "The Weird's having the arrows fired at you. Use your AI."

"How?"

"The same way you used it in the last game. That's how you made those jumps."

The music played on. A burning sensation followed as an arrow nicked his arm. In growing confusion, frustration, and fear, Alex shouted, "I didn't use my AI! What abou—"

"Get your AI to use the closest gravity generators to lift you. That's the easiest way to go over the wall."

Another arrow struck near Alex's feet and he jumped back. Alex had more learning to do and he needed to hurry. He looked frantically at Hymeron. "I don't understand. How can gravity lift me?"

Hymeron spoke quickly. "A gravity generator creates nuclei to pull you or an object toward them. Oh, and Alex, you might want to know you'll feel pain learning to sword fight."

Alex quickly looked at his stinging and bleeding arm. *Yeah, great news. Now, how do I work this AI? Up,* Alex thought. Nothing happened. His AI wasn't doing anything. *Maybe it can't lift anything.* A rock tore from the ground between his feet and hit him between the legs. Alex folded over in pain and closed his eyes. Grimacing, Alex thought. *The stupid thing was supposed to lift me up.* His feet left the ground, and he soared into the air. *Much better.* The pain ebbed and he smiled. *I like flying.* The moment after the thought, he was greeted by the view of a huge tree rapidly approaching. Reflexively, Alex curled into a ball.

"Ahhhh!" He screamed. Limbs snapped and leaves brushed past his face, until he came to a stop wedged between two branches. *Pain. Don't move me. Please don't move me.* Alex carefully shifted. Nothing hurt more. *Good, nothings broken.*

Hymeron called. "Are you okay?"

Bitterly he said, "Fine, I'm just fine."

Alex slowly climbed down. A groan escaped his lips as he stood and stretched. Alex moved out into a clearing. Carefully, he thought to the AI, *lift me straight up without hitting anything and don't move me any other way. Got that? Now lift me up.* He lifted smoothly off the ground going higher and higher. Alex looked around, sighing. This was better and the view was great. A sea shimmered in the distance. A forest stretched the other direction to the foot of tall snow-covered mountains. Gently he floated up, slowing down. He concentrated on not looking straight down. Moving his arms Alex discovered he could turn around. Preoccupied, he didn't notice starting to fall. Soon the wind began to whistle past. In his mind he thought, *uh AI thingy, you need to stop me.* Below the castle grew larger and larger as Alex fell.

"Ahhhhhhh!" *Stop! Stop me!*

~**********~

Alex stood in a forest. An unaccustomed weight hung from his hip. In front of him, Hheilea stood tied to a tree. *She looks worried.* A short scruffy man holding a sword stood between her and Alex. Legs wobbly from the fall, Alex collapsed on the grassy ground. A scabbard holding a sword dug into his calf muscle. Out of his confusion, he asked, "What happened?"

Hymeron said, "The Weird brought you here before you smashed into the ground. You need to get it together."

Hheilea screamed. "Get back up! He's going to hit you!"

The fighter ran at Alex. "Eeyah!"

Alex scrambled to his feet. The fighter charged. Wild hair whipped back from a face dominated by a gaping mouth with big square teeth. The fighter held a two-handed sword over his head. All of this and more Alex saw in a fraction of a second. Frantic, he dodged around a small bush.

Hymeron yelled at him. "Use your sword."

Still screaming his battle cry, the fighter charged through the bush. Alex leapt behind a tree. *I don't know how to —.* Something whistled past his ear to hit the tree with a thunk. He jumped back almost falling. The fighter pushed against the tree with a hand and ripped his weapon out of the wood. Alex yanked his own sword free of its scabbard as the fighter charged him again. *He's going to cut me in two.* In desperation Alex raised his sword above his head to catch the blow. A ringing clang testified of success. Dancing to the side, Alex dropped the point of his sword, allowing the fighter's sword to slide down his. *That worked. Now maybe....* Twisting his sword back at his attacker, Alex lunged at the fighter. He intended to skewer the figure, but a root caught his foot and he tumbled to the ground. The sword of the fighter pierced through the air at Alex's throat.

~**********~

"How did that go?" Hymeron asked.

"What? Where?" Now Alex stood in a grassy dell with Hymeron, Hheilea, and a tall man. A blue and orange butterfly fluttered by Alex toward the man, who wore a gray robe secured about the waist by a wide leather belt with a jewel-encrusted scabbard. It landed on the black pommel of the man's sword.

"Your instinct is good. You did a serviceable block," said the stranger with a harsh voice. "You need practice on your footwork. Tripping during an attack is very dangerous. Of course, instead of trying to block, you should've moved in close and gutted your attacker."

Alex stepped back from the gruff man. "Who are you?"

"I'm Weldon, the legendary sword master," Weldon said, rubbing a scraggly brown beard with one hand as he looked Alex up and down. He turned and looked at Hheilea, giving her an abbreviated bow. "I didn't know we had a young kimley woman with us. Am I training this boy to help protect you? He isn't going to be proficient for a long time. I could come out and be your knight."

Hymeron interrupted his sister's attempt to answer. "Please keep it a secret. No one's supposed to know about my sister. She's been in disguise as a younger boy. I don't know how or why the Weird took her disguise away." Then he added to Alex, "Weldon's a computer character."

Again, Weldon stood still stroking his chin, and absently spoke looking off into the distance. "Hmmm. I need to have a chat with the Weird about this."

Hheilea stomped forward, but her long, full dress snagged on a plant. Muttering under her breath, she tugged it free. "Thank you for offering to protect me. I'll think about it. I'm Hheilea and this is my brother, Hymeron."

Weldon said, "That dress isn't very practical for here. If the Weird insists on having you wear it, you could gird your loins."

"What?" she asked, perplexed.

Weldon removed his belt and with a series of movements gathered and moved his robe until he tied a knot in front of his waist. The robe still covered his torso, but from the waist down it now looked like a bulky diaper. "I have done this before to get my robe out of the way." Next, he turned to Alex. "What's your name?"

"Uh, Alex."

"Okay, Alex, pull out your sword, and I'll start your training."

"Alex watched, as Hheilea gathered the white dress up in front of her thighs. This pulled the white fabric snug against her backside.

A curt command came from Weldon. "Don't watch her."

Alex heard the words, but mesmerized by Hheilea he continued to watch. Something deep within him responded to both her and the music.

Weldon spoke again. Now his words were serious and firm. "Pull out your sword."

Alex tore his eyes away from Hheilea, ignoring the plea from somewhere inside his head to keep watching her. *What's up with this music? Not another alien....* He wrapped his hand around the sword's grip and slid the weapon out of the scabbard.

Weldon pulled out his own sword. "A sword is not a club. Don't grasp it like one. Hold it like this."

Alex shifted his grip a little. *What's going on with me? Am I going to respond to all alien girls this way?*

"You're still holding it like a club. Use your index finger and thumb to do most of the gripping. Keep the cutting edge of the blade towards me and the point aimed at my eyes."

Alex looked into Weldon's light brown eyes. *At least I can look at his eyes without feeling goofy. I've got to focus on this training. What's happening to me?*

"Good. Watch your opponent's eyes." Weldon shook his head. "Don't hold the sword so far from your body. You won't have any strength in your parry or attack. Keep the arm bent and hold the sword in closer to your body. Remember the farther the blade is turned away from your enemy, the more time it takes to parry or attack. Now walk with me, stay ready to attack or defend." Weldon started walking to the side, forcing Alex to walk sideways to keep facing him.

Alex stumbled and fell over some logs. "Where did the logs come from?" Alex asked, getting back to his feet and picking up his sword.

"Good question," Weldon said. "Did your eyes see them, before your feet found them? Use your eyes. You have to watch me and see where you are placing your feet. Otherwise you'll fall and die. Let's do that again."

Alex tried again and again, constantly adding to his collection of bruises. Hheilea had disappeared. Hymeron sat in a tree yelling words of encouragement, until Weldon told him to shut up or leave. He stayed, but Alex could still hear the occasional laugh.

At lunchtime, Hheilea didn't respond to their calls. Alex said, "Shouldn't we check on her?"

"Ha," Hymeron said. "This is the Weird. She's fine and you'll be better off not looking for her."

Later when the guys were preparing to eat dinner, they called to her again. Alex yelled, "Come on, Hheilea. You have to be getting hungry."

Hymeron said, "When she's mad, it's best just to leave her alone. I'm going to get some more firewood."

She's mad? Alex started to respond. "Wh—"

Weldon followed Hymeron. "I'll help you."

Not to long after the two of them disappeared into the woods, Alex heard someone crashing through the bushes and then Hheilea stomped into the clearing. *Okay, she's mad, but I've got a right to some answers.* Alex quickly stepped toward her, but she turned away. Reaching out a hand, he touched her shoulder and said, "What's going on?"

Hheilea knocked his hand away and spat words at him. "Nothing's going on."

Nothing's going on? She doesn't know the half of my problems, but one I think she should know is this music stuff. Alex paused, trying hard not to yell. He said, "I understand you're upset, but...."

Hheilea shoved at his chest, interrupting him. "You don't understand anything."

She lifted her hands to shove him again as she glared. He looked back into her eyes. Notes of music rose and fell, like the crashing of waves, and he shook. The seconds seemed to stretch into hours. *She's shaking too.*

Alex reached out and grasped her arms. "You hear this music too. What does it mean?"

"It doesn't mean anything!" she yelled at him, twisting out of his grasp.

At this point, Weldon strode into the clearing and tossed an armful of wood to the ground. He pulled his sword out and pointed to Hheilea. "Take that sword the Weird is offering you and try to hit me."

Alex watched Hheilea snatch the sword hanging in the air and charge, slashing at Weldon. The sword master backed up, just blocking her blows. They circled the fire, filling the air with the sound of ringing blows. Alex grasped the pommel of his own sword. *This I understand. There's nothing I can do about Twarbie, and now I've got something going on with Hheilea, and she won't talk about it. I would love to run around screaming and slashing at something, anything. Except if I do, I'll probably give away the secret of Twarbie being in the Weird. Instead, I have to act like I hardly care about anything.* He gritted his teeth. *The British spy always seemed to do well in the long run by staying calm, but trying to be that way is frustrating.* Hymeron charged out of the woods, stopping by Alex.

Finally, Hheilea dropped her sword and leaned on her knees, gasping for breath. Weldon slid his sword into its scabbard and untied a leather flask. He offered it to Hheilea. "Here, rinse out your mouth, spit, and take a sip."

Accepting the offer she poured some of the liquid into her mouth, swished it around, and spit into the flames, where it sizzled. Lifting the flask again, she took a sip, swallowed, and then took another. She handed it back to Weldon. "Thanks. I feel better now. Where's the food?"

Putting an arm around her shoulder, Weldon led her to the food.

Alex screamed to himself. The worst of it was he knew the Weird would wake him for his regular morning time with Twarbie. Lately, his sessions with her had started with various scenarios which required him to react instantly. Would she be waiting to attack me or have breakfast with me? *What's it going to be this time?*

~**********~

Alex stood on a wobbling platform surrounded by lapping water.

The Weird said, "The scene I've put you in has you and Twarbie on a sinking island. It's surrounded by a solution which will burn your skin. The island will sink, unless only one of you is on it."

Alex looked at the nearby shore. *It isn't far. I don't know how Twarbie will react to this. Everything she's been taught goes against this situation. It won't hurt long.* He took one quick look at a very uncertain Twarbie standing with a pale face, slightly open mouth, and breathing really fast. Closing his eyes, Alex dove in. *Ahhh the pain!* He almost opened his mouth to scream. With skin boiling in agony, he beat at the liquid. After an eternity of pain and a few strokes, he felt his hands strike the shore. Quickly, he crawled onto the shore. Immediately a holo-field formed around him. The pain died away.

Beside him, Twarbie screamed at him. "How could you?!"

"What? You weren't out there?" Alex stood up and looked back just in time to see a duplicate Twarbie still standing, before the decoy disappeared.

Words ripped out of Twarbie's mouth. "The Weird had me on the shore. It wouldn't let me say anything. I tried to call out. I could see your skin blistering." She backed up, holding her hands out screaming, "No! No! No!"

She turned and jumped into the water. For a second, shock kept Alex standing and watching as she screamed and gagged. Pink foam bubbled around her mouth. Alex jumped feet-first back in. This time he screamed in pain, even as he found footing and struggled to grab the thrashing girl. Finally, he just wrapped his arms around her even as the liquid splashed into his mouth, and more pain added to his overloaded circuits. Crying in pain, confusion, rage, and concern, he fought to carry the still thrashing body out of the burning liquid. Stumbling in agony, he forged ahead. Finally, he collapsed onto the shore. He tried to call out her name, but only a hoarse croak came out. *Why had the Weird put them into this and why, why, why had Twarbie jumped in? It was insanity.*

The Weird said, "Drink this."

Alex looked up to see a blue vial of liquid. The physical pain had gone, but unbearable emotions ripped at him. Alex snatched it out of the air, but the shaking of his hand threatened to spill all the liquid. *I've got to control myself.* He started to drink, but stopped, and looked down at the unconscious girl.

"You first. Then help her."

Alex tipped the vial up and as he drank saw another vial appear. Instantly his throat felt better. Dropping his empty one, he snatched the other out of the air. A wave of light-headedness struck, and he gasped trying to get the strength to continue.

"Take it slow. She isn't in pain."

Alex looked down. Twarbie's bleeding blisters were gone. Tenderly, carefully he tipped her head and pressed the vial against her lips. "Twarbie, drink this. It'll help."

She must've heard, because her lips parted. He slowly poured the blue substance into her mouth. Gulping she managed to swallow, even as some ran out of her mouth. The blue traced flowing lines across her skin. Alex threw the vial away. *I wish I could make the Weird feel our pain.*

The Weird said, "Do you know why she jumped in?"

"Of course not." *I hate this computer. How can it be so heartless?* Bitterly he laughed at that brainless thought. After all, it was just a computer or a program.

"Did you mean it, weeks ago, when you told Twarbie give me some time to get to know you?"

Alex looked down at the very alien girl. *Cramming his emotions down, he tried to speak calmly.* "Hey, can you hear us?"

The girl nodded her head.

"Why did you jump in?"

The answer was very soft and quiet. "The pain of seeing you dive in.... I've never had... pain like that before. I had to jump in."

All Alex could do was shake his head at the crazy answer. *She doesn't make sense.*

What she said next really shocked Alex. "You're so alien to me. I know why the Weird didn't have me out there. It knows me. In a situation like that, I've been trained not to think. I would've just shoved you in. When you dove in, it shocked and hurt me. It made me think of what you said about the son of your God. Sacrificing yourself for another is so alien to how I've been raised. I... The worst was... when I realized I would've hurt more... if I had pushed you in. What's happing to me?"

~**********~

In the following weeks, Alex tried multiple times to talk about what was happening to him. He asked Hymeron about the music and about the danger Hheilea faced. Each time Hymeron avoided the questions. Many times Alex caught Hheilea looking at him, but immediately she would turn away. She refused his efforts to talk to her. *They're being so stupid. They know what's going on, but they refuse to talk about it.*

Late one evening, Alex walked off into the woods by himself trying to find some peace from the turmoil inside.

"Hard to deal with everything?"

"What? Oh, it's you." Alex spoke to the Weird, really not wanting the intrusion and ignoring the question. Then Alex jumped as a voice spoke in his head.

|I could talk to you privately. Just think in your head, AI, I want to talk to the Weird. Your AI will make the connection, and I'll hear what you have to say. By the way, you should talk to your AI more.|

Alex stopped walking. He considered the idea and carefully tried it out. |That would be convenient at times. It's also another thing I'll have to remember not to let the kimleys know I understand.|

|That's how you do it. If you want to talk with me about anything, just use your AI.|

|Right now, I just want to be left alone.|

Continuing on through the forest, he was grateful the Weird stopped interrupting his attempt to find some peace. Still thoughts of the two alien girls intruded. Finally, Alex gave up the effort and went to sleep, knowing when he woke up it would be to spend time with Twarbie, the other part of his troubles. He didn't want to think about her.

Trying not to figure Twarbie out left his mind to stew over the problem in a dream. Alex stood with the alien girl. Together they watched as first Alex and later Twarbie jumped into the burning solution. Dream Twarbie said, "The Weird wanted to give you more emotional pain. It says pain will help your learning proceed faster. I don't understand what the Weird's doing. This scene with the caustic liquid is strange. Why would you believe I jumped in? You're confusing. Still, there's something about you which attracts me. It makes playing with your emotions more fun. Too bad you're so alien, and I know nothing about how to love."

On a warm afternoon, Alex stood with a club, knee-deep in the smashed remains of dozens of melons. Both of the kimleys had been gone for almost twenty minutes. Weldon sat on a branch above him. "Now that you've gotten some of your anger out, do you want to talk about what's going on?"

Alex shifted his grip and smashed another melon. |Weird, make the melons tougher.| "Nothing's going on." *How could he understand?*

Weldon dropped a melon. Alex twisted and swung overhand connecting with a satisfying thunk to knock it away. Quickly Alex shifted his feet to keep his balance, but a thought almost caused him to fall. |Weird? Was that something I shouldn't have asked you to do?|

|No, I could've done it on my own.|

The sword master tossed a handful of smaller melons which curved through the air to come at Alex from different directions. "Alex, you should recognize anger can be a help in battle to fuel your resolution and force, but at the same time anger and other emotions must be dealt with appropriately or they'll cause you trouble."

Alex gritted his teeth. *What does he know about emotions?* He cocked the club over a shoulder and grunted as he swung at the closest melon. With a thunk the melon arced up and away. *Ha, home run.*

Multiple thumps and Alex staggered. The other melons tap danced against the back of his head.

"Those melons are like the emotions raging in you from your time with Twarbie and the kimleys."

"What?" Alex interrupted. *How does he know?*

"You're actually handling it surprisingly well, but you need to talk about it," Weldon said.

"I don't need to talk about it," Alex said. *How could he help me?*

Weldon said, "Okay. Whatever you want. Take care of these melons coming out of the woods at you, and that'll be enough strength training for today. Next, we'll work with swords, but with something new added in. I'm happy with your progress. You're starting to anticipate my attacks. That's very important for any form of fighting. Remember to always watch your opponent's eyes. This will help you prepare for their attack. I haven't figured out why at times your ability to anticipate an attack is worse. For example, you weren't doing very good anticipating melons during the last twenty minutes, but those last few you did great. Also, you need to be quicker with the tierce block. We'll work on it today. I don't know what your schedule is like, but when you have time, make sure you come back. Have your AI bring up Weldon, the Sword Master. In a year, I might be willing to admit I taught you."

"Okay," Alex gasped as he smashed melons flying at him from all directions. Glimpsing Hheilea returning with her brother, he almost missed the last one. *There's that distracting music again.* Covered in melon gore, he added. "Is there something I can wipe my face off with?"

"Better than wipe it off," Weldon gruffly said. "Just get rid of it like this."

All of the melon gore disappeared from Alex. Where he had been wading in gore, he now stood balanced on a log.

"You could've done the same with your AI. It can communicate with the Weird." Weldon levitated into the sky. "Follow me."

Alex stood on the ground looking up at Weldon. *They keep talking about my working with the AI, but it doesn't talk to me. I could get the Weird to help, but the kimleys are watching, and that would give away my time with Twarbie.* "I can't get up there."

"What?" Weldon shouted. His face turned a dark red, and his eyeballs bulged out. Swooping out of the sky, he shook a fist in Hymeron's face. "You've brought me a wet-behind-the-ear-kid, who can't even use his AI! This is ridiculous. Come back when he's ready." Weldon vanished.

Alex threw his club down. "Doesn't he know the Weird is in control of my training? It isn't our fault."

"He'll get over it," Hymeron said.

Alex glanced at Hheilea and turned away as the song attacked his emotions. Alex had learned to look at Hheilea only briefly to keep the song from getting too strong. "Is Weldon really just a computer character? He has such strong emotions. It's like he's real."

In an exasperated tone of voice, Hheilea said, "Of course he's real. Don't you pay attention at all? Remember him eating fish and bread with us around the fire?"

Alex held his hands up in puzzlement. "What? Either he's a computer character or real."

Hheilea took a deep breath and answered in a calmer voice. "Look, he's just another type of AI. Some people call them RE because they have a real existence. You need to talk more to your AI. It won't respond much at first, but it will react to simple requests, such as, 'find a local gravity generator and lift me.' You just need to learn how to define what you mean by 'lift me.' Your AI is a baby. Working with it can be interesting."

Hheilea laughed before she continued. "Over time it will learn and as a result respond to you better. Also, it grows in abilities to fit who you are. I've heard of a few people who manage to develop incredible AI, but we haven't seen anyone do that."

Hymeron stood up. "You're going to play a new game. It's similar to the first game, but first, we should eat and you need rest."

Alex didn't like the idea of sleep. With it would come a new day and trouble with Twarbie. Yet, he eagerly went to sleep. *Maybe she and the Weird can help me with this AI thing.*

~**********~

Alex woke to a gentle breeze blowing all around him. At first, he just rested with his eyes shut enjoying the comfort of lying in—. A number of things struck him at once. *I can't feel the hammock. The breeze is blowing all around me, underneath and above. Heart pounding, Alex's eyes popped wide open. He screamed. "Aaaaah!"*

A bubbly, cheerful laugh startled him just enough to free him, a bit, from his fear. Cutting off the screaming, but still breathing hard, Alex looked around. Next to him, Twarbie sat cross-legged, floating in the air and laughing. In surprise, he asked, "What's going on?"

With another laugh, Twarbie said, "The Weird wants you to get comfortable using your AI to move through the air."

She's laughing. Alex said, "I've never heard you laugh like this before."

She giggled. "It also wanted me to lighten up."

She leaned forward and in a stage whisper said, "It gave me a drug." She giggled again and waved a finger at him. "But you don't get any."

Alex grinned. "This is a nice change."

In an almost normal voice, Twarbie said, "Yes. I agree. Yesterday, the Weird tried to help me understand leaving one's culture, family, home, and god. It told me the story of Ruth. She left everything she had known and stayed with her mother-in-law and her people. Eventually things worked out for her. Also, a story about Anush, a young teenager, given by her people as a bride to seal a treaty with another tribe. Her new life was much better, but even though everyone treated her like a princess, she couldn't adjust to the new culture. And... well this time with you in the Weird has been too crazy. I don't know if my life can be like Ruth's or—."

In a pained voice she added, "I don't think I should've talked about that. Weird, can I have some more of the drug?"

120

"Just a little. I'm worried about how you'll react."

A small purple cloud formed in front of her and she sucked it out of the air. A big smile spread across her face. "Thanks, I feel better."

Twarbie held her hands over her head and spun head-over-heels. "Weeeeee. This is fun. Ask your baby AI, reeaal nicely, to use a gravity generator to pull you feet. —" She giggled and then very slowly said, "I... meant... your... feet. Weeeee. This is fun. Be sure ask baby only use generator to start you spinning. Weee. Otherwise, it'll pull you through the air by the feet. Weeee." Twarbie stopped spinning. Her face looked a bit green to Alex.

And she threw up. Fortunately, the spewed vomit missed Alex.

"Weird, I think you gave her too much of that drug."

The Weird laughed. "You think so? I'm recording this and maybe I'll use it to blackmail her."

"Is that a good idea? I suspect she'd find a way to disconnect you, if you tried."

"Oooh naughty Weird and naughty tummy. Can I have something for my tummy and maybe some more of this feel-good drug?"

A soberer Weird answered. "The blackmail idea was a bad joke. I hope she doesn't remember it. And no, Twarbie, I don't think more of this drug would be a good idea. You're going to have to learn to release the tension from your life without a drug. I suspect you could get reliant on this drug and that would be bad. For one thing, you can't act like this outside."

Tears started to run down Twarbie's face. "That's not nice. You wanted this to be fun and relaxing for us, and then you mentioned my real life.

Alex carefully asked his AI to move him just a little. With a jerk, he glided toward Twarbie.

A contrite Weird said, "I'm sorry, Twarbie."

She laughed. "It's okay. I can't stay sad or even get upset." Twarbie leaned forward and grasped Alex by the hand. Gently she pulled on him. "Come on. Let's play."

Chapter Fourteen
The First Fight

In the new game, Alex stood on a grassy platform next to a pile of snow. Around the three of them floated other platforms in all directions. Scattered about were big tubs of mud, buckets of water, and more snow. Far below he could see the ground. The kimleys stood on their own platforms. Again, Hheilea looked the part of a boy. She grinned at Alex and then turned away, even as Alex looked away to quiet the music. Over both her and Hymeron's heads floated green holograms with the number zero.

Hymeron tossed a snow ball from hand to hand. He threw it, hitting Alex.

"Hey," Alex said, reaching down for ammunition to return fire.

"Look up," Hheilea said, pointing over Alex's head.

Above Alex flashed a yellow-green hologram with the number one displayed.

"When that number reaches sixty, you lose. Dunking you in a tub of mud is thirty points. If you hit the ground, it's game over," Hymeron said. "The color also changes from green to orange as you get hit. Good luck." The kimleys started belting Alex with snowballs.

Alex jumped, aiming for another platform, trying to get away, but missed and plummeted toward the ground. Quickly, he commanded his AI to boost him with a gravity generator so he could land on a distant platform. Just before he hit the ground, a ferocious jerk to his body signaled the change in direction. Reaching the platform, he tried to stand, but had too much forward momentum and tumbled off the far side of it. It didn't matter much to Alex that his flashing hologram

122

turned orange. Landing face first onto a grass platform took precedence.

~**********~

Two weeks later, still in the same scene, Alex jumped toward a platform. |AI, flip this platform to block Hheilea's attack.|

Hheilea fired snowballs at him, but his grass platform flipped up just in time. Alex said, "Hah—I blocked you this time." |Good job, AI.|

"Look up," Hheilea said, laughing as Alex tipped his head back just in time to get a face full of snow.

That evening, Hheilea and Hymeron sat beside Alex, holding sticks, and roasting a marshmallow-type treat over a lava flow. A barren mountain rose into an orange sky. From the mountain top, a fountain of lava shot a thousand feet into the air. The crescent of a giant planet hung above them filling most of the sky. But Alex didn't pay any attention to the amazing views or how the Weird made it all work. He concentrated on talking with his AI. It didn't answer, except in no, yes, and a very uncertain uh. What still surprised him were the tones to the answers. The AI sounded childish or childlike.

Hheilea said to him, "You're quiet tonight. Are you getting discouraged?"

"I just want to be done and get back to the flock. We've been in the Weird's world forever. I'm still puzzled about how it makes these worlds, and I really don't understand what the Weird is. You've said it's a computer, but other times, it sounds like another AI." *I'll have to work with the Weird for what my AI can't or won't do.*

A bubble in the lava popped, throwing tendrils of lava up into the air. Hheilea jerked her treat back. One of the tendrils hit Hymeron's marshmallow treat melting into it, and in a second, flames covered the remains of the treat. Hymeron tossed the stick onto the lava, where it burst into flames. He held a hand out, and another stick with a marshmallow treat appeared. With a long sigh, Hymeron looked at Alex. "The

Weird is another AI, and it's in a computer of its own. You're supposed to figure your AI out on your own, but you're taking forever. Your AI interfaces with other computers."

Alex started to respond and then stopped. *I hate sounding like a whiner, but I don't want them to know how good I'm doing.* "I'm trying, but you're making it too hard."

"I'm sorry. Don't give up. You're getting better," Hheilea said.

Hymeron poked his sister. "Stop being such a softy. He's pretending. Trying to get us to take it easier and give him a chance to beat us."

Alex grinned. When Hheilea looked at him he tried to hide it with a pretend yawn. She gazed at him in surprise, and he shrugged and winked at her. Hheilea jumped to her feet and tossed her stick down. "Come on, Hymeron, let's go to our room and get some sleep."

"Okay. I'm coming. Just don't act so bossy." Hymeron pulled his sticky treat off the stick he held and popped it into his mouth.

Deep into plans for the next day, Alex didn't even notice they had left.

The next day started as usual with Twarbie waking him up. Alex just lay looking up at the rosy colored sky and listening to the distant rumble of the volcano. *Today, I'll finish with my AI training and should get back to the sword training. Hopefully, I'll get to leave soon.* A fragrance caught his attention. Even through the slightly sulfurous smell of the lava it was strong and clear. The odors weren't the flowery scents of Twarbie. He was used to those and hardly noticed them anymore. This was the smell of fresh bread and cooked fruit of some kind. He sat up in his hammock and spotted Twarbie sitting next to the lava flow holding something golden on a long stick over the heat. As he watched, juices dripped from the food to evaporate as they fell. *Today should be great. I've gotten my AI to cooperate.*

"Good, you're finally awake. I hope you like this. I asked the Weird to let me cook breakfast for you."

"What is it?" Alex swung his legs over the side, stood up, and moving closer to Twarbie, sat on a rock.

Twarbie pulled the stick back and started to slide the foot-long, golden brown item onto a plate. "Ow!"

Flames erupted as the food fell into the lava. A small pink cloud enveloped her fingers and Twarbie shrugged her shoulders. "Oh well, it was just mine. It's a very old recipe of my people. We call it forbidden fruit. It's very delicious. I checked with the Weird and your metabolism can deal with it."

With her other hand, she picked up a different plate and brought it to him. The item on the plate smelled tantalizingly good. A blue juice had leaked to form a small pool around the food. "This one should be cool enough to eat. Try it."

Alex reached for it and carefully picked the food up. Odors tantalized his nose and mouth. He inhaled savoring the aroma. "What's in this?"

"It's a frozen foot-long berry from our home world wrapped in very sticky bread dough. Cooked right, the inside is all soft and warm. I kinda cheated and had the Weird help me get the temperature right."

Alex tentatively bit into one end of it. The crust was crispy giving way to a soft warm bread and then the middle. Overcome by the flavor, Alex gasped with his mouth full. "Wow."

"You're going to drip." Twarbie leaned over and wiped some juice off his chin.

After swallowing, Alex asked, "Why is it called forbidden fruit?"

"It's one thing we resist our God about. Our God wants us to deny ourselves, but Winkles can't give it up. Sometimes a serious effort is made by the leadership, but then they give in."

"You lost yours. Do you want a bite of mine?"

Twarbie sat down beside him. "I was hoping you would ask. An odd thing about this.... It's better shared. When my mom and I share one, I almost think she loves me, but that can't be."

After the last shared bites, Alex gazed at Twarbie. *How much longer before we both leave the Weird? What's going to...? I'm going to miss her and this time together. Is she blushing?*

Twarbie turned away from his gaze. "The Weird told me this will probably be our last morning together."

Alex didn't know what to say. "Uhmmm."

"You're supposed to tell me how you'll miss me." Twarbie looked back at Alex.

Her face is a bit red. Her eyes.... Is she going to cry?

"Are you even thinking of what to say?" Then much quieter she added, as if to herself. "It's okay. You don't have to say anything, but after you leave here don't try to find me or help me. Remember if the other winkles know you're my friend, they'll force me to torture you to death, and I can't stand that thought. I'll just be how I'm expected to be."

Alex opened his mouth to argue, but Twarbie continued talking. "There's something I want to do with you before we say goodbye."

What?

Twarbie leaned closer and grasped Alex's face with her hands. Their lips met and the crazy sweetness filled his mouth. Dizziness threatened to overwhelm him. He reached with his arms intending on crushing her to him and never letting go, but she wasn't there.

Again they stood on the small wobbling island surrounded by the dangerous liquid. Except this time, Alex stumbled and fell to the ground. Looking up he saw Twarbie gazing back at him. She gave him a determined smile and turned toward the water. *What's she going to do? She won't. Why?*

Twarbie dove into the water with a splash. Alex scrambled to all fours and launched himself out to help her. He landed painfully, face down on the ground. Tumbling he came to a stop. A few steps away, Twarbie lay on the ground surrounded by a pink cloud quickly changing to blue. Even as he clambered to his feet she sat up and smiled at him.

"What? Why did you?" He closed the distance.

"I think that's one of the things I love about you. Even when you're so confused and uncertain you charge."

Love? Alex froze.

"The Weird helped me see how and why the two heroes, Stick and Gursha, risked their lives to save others. Also, the Weird showed me movies from Earth to help me understand love. I watched a whole list of movies. It Happened One Night, Casablanca, Singin' in the Rain, The Adventures of Robin Hood, and others. I understood Scarlett O'Hara the best, but I cried myself to sleep at her loss. She had a God which drove her to pain and loss too."

Alex stepped toward Twarbie at the sound of hurt in her voice.

In one smooth move, she rose to her feet and languorously stretched as Alex stared with parted lips. *She's like a cat when she does that. An incredible... This isn't good. I'm not like that spy. I can't just. I should ask the Weird to put dry clothes on her. Why hasn't she? Wait, the caustic liquid would still be burning her. Her clothes are wet with just water and on purpose. She knows—*

Slowly, Twarbie stepped up to Alex and lightly ran her fingers over his shoulders. "You've gotten so muscular in the past months. Then he noticed for the first time her teeth were not just white and even, but also pointed and sharp looking. *What's happening? What's she doing?*

She moved lightly, pressing against him as her fingers played down his back. Her head tipped back, and as he looked down he saw her swallow and close her eyes. She stretched up and pressed her lips firmly against his. He responded. His arms crushed her to him and he kissed her back. There wasn't any overpowering sweetness, but he wanted to keep kissing her. *Something's wrong. I need to....* He shifted his arms and grasped her by the waist. Hating himself, he pushed her back. Their lips separated and her eyes opened. *Is that a tear going down her cheek?*

Twarbie's lips parted. "Don't hate me."

Alex found himself puckering up... *She's controlling me again, for another kiss.*

She puckered up and leaned against him. Breathing heavy, her hands explored his back. Quietly she said, "Silly human, so easy to control."

Alex stared at her, wanting the kiss, but not wanting to be forced. At the same time he screamed in his head. *What's she doing?! This isn't the Twarbie I've come to know.*

The girl tipped her head, stretched up, and bit him on the chin. With a gasp at the pain, he managed to step back. She licked her lips. "You have fought back. I've had fun with you. Goodbye."

She was gone. Alex fell to his knees. *What? Why?* Agony tore at him and unshed tears burned in his eyes. *That wasn't Twarbie. I've been with her months. How could she?*

The Weird's voice broke into his torment. "You need to get yourself under control. Soon you'll be with Hheilea and Hymeron."

Anger raged in Alex. "I'm sick of your games. I'm not going to cooperate anymore. Get me out of here."

"This will be your last day and then you'll rejoin your flock. You've learned things here that you needed."

Sarcasm and anger filled his voice. "Yeah. I've learned to not trust any alien or AI." *I want to get out of here and forget about all of this, including Twarbie.*

~***********~

Hheilea stood next to Hymeron on a platform. Again, they encouraged Alex to gain a better understanding of how to use his AI, even as they worked at beating him. Hheilea shouted at Alex, "You're moving much better through the air. I think you've made a breakthrough with your AI. Did you practice last night?"

Alex didn't answer. It was time to put his plan into action. |AI, have the Weird make me disappear, and make an image of me appear over by Hymeron. Do everything just as we rehearsed last night.|

Hheilea asked, "Where did Alex go?"

Hymeron shouted, "He's over here." He began throwing snowballs at Alex, but then stopped and threw his hands up. "He's just standing. What's he trying to do? We're going to be stuck in here forever."

Hheilea joined him and said, "No, Alex is up to something."

Hymeron said, "Are you—."

Alex disappeared. Hheilea gasped and looked around trying to spot him. "Where did he go?"

Alex chuckled to himself as began throwing balls of mud at Hheilea and Hymeron. He stood close to them, but the Weird had instructions to keep him invisible to the kimleys.

"Over here!" Hymeron shouted, jumping onto a platform to escape the blizzard of mud. Hheilea jumped after him. Something shoved her, and she crashed into Hymeron.

"Aaahh! You're knocking me off." Hymeron slid toward the edge.

Alex told his AI, tip that platform. Don't allow Hymeron or Hheilea to interface with the Weird.

"No, the platform's tipping us off." With a splash she landed in cold soupy mud with her brother.

"I hope I wasn't too rough on you little kids," Alex said from above them.

Covered in mud, Hheilea stood with her fists on her hips. "I'm not a little kid." And then she laughed. "You did it."

Alex stood looking back at her. His triumphant feeling faded, his face turned warm, and he mumbled. "No, you're definitely not a little kid." Jumping off his platform, he flipped through the air. "I'm finally starting to enjoy this. You know, I've really gotten to like you two. This training has been fun, and I'm feeling much stronger. But I'd like to return to my flock."

"I wish you could," Hymeron said. "Unfortunately, the Weird says you need to go back to the castle and rescue the fair maiden." He grumbled, "At least no RE that can leave the computer world has seen Hhy is actually Hheilea, except for Weldon." At that Hymeron snorted, "Lucky for us, he doesn't know how to be anything but morally high minded, follow all rules, and be good. No wonder the deems beat him."

~**********~

They returned to the forest, beside the castle wall. A weight at his waist caused Alex to glance down. A grey and black scabbard with a sword hung from his waist. Light reflected off a deep purple crystal, set in the pommel. The hilt was all black, including the guard.

Alex gave his AI a command, and he rose smoothly to the top of the wall. With his AI interfacing with the Weird, he found the archers and had the Weird create sticky rope that bound itself around them. This was going to be easy, Alex thought. Another command to his AI sent him toward the top of the tower, where the slim young woman in white waited.

A familiar soft sweet voice called from the top of the tower. "Alex, save me and we can get out of here."

Oof — The air squeezed from his lungs as he collided with an invisible barrier.

A guttural cry from below drew his eyes down. A huge black figure stood in front of the door to the tower. Two big scaly wings flapped from the figure's back. Even from this distance, Alex could see its blazing red eyes. He raised a hand and beckoned to Alex. "Are you ready to challenge me?"

"What are you?" Alex asked, looking down toward the base of the tower. *It's a gaahr, that beast Twarbie looked like. I shouldn't continue to protect her. It would be fun to surprise the kimleys with my knowledge.*

The black figure's whip-like tail lashed behind it. A big, toothy grin creased the figure's face. "I'm a gaahr, one of the deems. We are the most powerful creatures of the universe. My name is Gagugugul. You are doomed."

Alex laughed at the pompous statement.

Alex ordered his AI to wrap this gaahr in sticky ropes. Momentarily the ropes appeared around monster and then disappeared.

The gaahr stood dressed in only a dark-red and gold harness. Some areas of its body were blurred as if out of focus. A necklace hung from his neck. "You can't defeat me with that kind of trick. I work with the Weird."

With a clawed hand, Gagugugul drew a huge sword from a scabbard. "I hope Weldon taught you how to fight with a sword, little boy. I want to have fun defeating you."

Placing a hand on the pommel of his sword, Alex drifted slowly down. The gaahr stretched out his thirty-foot wings and rose to meet him. The monster was easily twice the size of

Alex. He paused, trying to control his voice as he faced the terror. "I think I'll call you Gargle. How do you know Weldon?" *How can I defeat him? He's over eight-feet tall. I've got to watch out for that tail.*

"We fight together sometimes," Gargle said. "I like him."

Hheilea said in a voice full of concern. "Alex, be careful. You can't trust deems."

Alex glanced up at her and then away needing to keep his focus.

Gargle laughed and said, "A young kimley woman, she has a problem."

"What do you mean?" Alex demanded.

"The Weird knows even if you don't," Gargle said, lifting his head he hollered at Hheilea. "A green crystal will help you!"

This deem didn't fit Alex's idea of what a deem would be. "I thought deems are terrible creatures. You look fearsome but sound quite reasonable."

"Well, you see, for now, I'm a tame deem locked inside the computers," Gargle said.

"Then step aside," Alex said, "and I won't have to hurt you."

Gargle laughed. "You insult me by your offer. You're ignorant. In this crazy world of the Weird, fire still burns." He roared, "I am a deem! I look forward to tasting your flesh."

Tasting my flesh? A shudder ran down Alex's spine. "I'm not afraid of you. You sound like a buffoon."

"Then prove it," Gargle said. "Pull your little toothpick out. Let's start this dance." Gargle opened his mouth wide and laughed a tremendous bellow of a laugh.

Alex paused. *A big melon would fit in his mouth.* Squaring his shoulders, he slid his sword out of its scabbard. Somebody else, another kimley, stood in front of him, dressed in a white loose fitting shirt and blue satiny pants. He was almost as tall as Alex. Distracted by the new arrival, he heard Gargle roar in the background. "The Weird is cheating!" Gargle fell back. "It gave you a *string-sword.*"

"Who are you?" Alex asked, puzzled.

In Alex's head he heard the kimley say, *Curse your luck.*

Another voice in Alex's head spoke. *He's Maleky, Julia's boss.*

Alex almost dropped his sword as memories long repressed swirled in his mind, and said out loud. "What's going on?"

The second voice spoke in his head. *Don't drop the sword. I'm your subconscious. Holding the sword allows me to speak directly to you and allows you to see Maleky. I've been battling him all alone, but now we can get rid of him. Attack him.*

Alex tentatively moved into the guard position, his right arm was slightly bent with the sword tip pointed at Maleky's eyes. His left hand he held back at his waist, prepared to grapple his opponent's sword arm. The sword glowed along the cutting edge leaving behind a trail of light, as it cut through the air. Alex slashed and stabbed at the air in front of him.

Maleky drew another sword, awkwardly copying Alex's position. His sword glowed a brilliant white on the cutting edge too and left behind a trail of light.

In Alex's head, his subconscious kept yelling. *Attack, get rid of Maleky"* Alex remembered Weldon telling him, when you attack never hesitate. Watching his opponent's eyes, Alex told his AI to move him forward. Maleky's eyes widened. Alex attacked.

Maleky gave a yelp and moved backwards. At the same time he swung his sword in front of himself, trying to block Alex's attack. With a twist of his wrist, Alex avoided the block and slashed at Maleky's torso. The kimley moved back just enough, but Alex's sword effortlessly sliced through the billowing shirt. Part of the kimley's shirt hung from where Alex had cut it.

Alex's subconscious crowed. *You almost had him. He's in your mind and knew when you were starting your attack. Keep after him. Don't give him a chance.*

"What are you doing?" Hheilea asked.

"What?" Alex asked, stopping to look around.

The sound of wings flapping caused him to look down. Gargle attacked from below, slashing at Alex's legs.

"Look-out!" Shouted two external voices and two internal voices.

Alex started to have his AI lift him upside down, when his feet flipped up over his head. *I got it for you.* A voice in his head told him. *What?* Everything spun for Alex. He slashed with his sword. Light trailed in an arc as the blade descended at the rising Gargle.

Wings beating frantically, Gargle tried to switch course. His blade rose in a block against Alex's attack. A ringing snap sounded the moment the light-blazing edge of Alex's sword sliced into and broke off his opponents. The gaahr retreated, dropping back, below, and away.

Panting, Alex looked back at Maleky. The kimley smiled at him and gave him a nod of approval. The subconscious voice again encouraged Alex to go after Maleky.

"But he warned me," Alex said aloud.

His subconscious answered back in his head. *But he's constantly giving you bad ideas. He's working off what Julia impressed into your mind. He's trying to finish getting you to think of yourself first. My working against him has made Maleky upset. I guess this isn't the way it was supposed to be. When he tries to encourage you to be different, these words come back to me. We must fight first to be what we would be."*

Alex hung in the air, troubled, and indecisive. His subconscious added. *He and Julia are keeping you from thinking of Sammy's situation, and he wants you to take advantage of A'idah and Hheilea.*

Hearing these words in his mind, Alex started to hold the sword like a club instead of a deadly tool. Eyes narrowed, he began to move through the air toward Maleky.

Maleky backed up, talking a steady stream of words. *You better watch out for Gargle. Julia and I are doing what's best for you. Putting yourself first is the best way to survive life. Knowing your future would make it easier. Others don't matter.*

Hymeron yelled from a distance, "What are you doing? Gargle's in the other direction!"

Maleky's words pounded at him. *I could help you understand Hheilea. I know what's going on. This could be a wonderful situation. You could use....*

Maleky lost the opportunity to speak the rest of the words, as Alex fell upon him with the sword. Anger brushed aside his recent training. He smashed at Maleky. There was no attack, retreat, parry, or riposte, as he'd been taught.

Some blows Maleky managed to dodge, others he frantically blocked, sparks of light flying as the two swords met. Still he was injured once and then twice. With each injury to Maleky, a strange feeling of turbulence in Alex's mind began.

"He's fighting someone," Gargle said, and then laughed adding. "I think someone's in his mind."

In desperation Maleky flew at Gargle with Alex right behind. Maleky didn't stop, but flew right through Gargle to hover behind him. Alex didn't stop either, but flew right at Gargle. His sword beat down at the fearsome, black creature.

"You're going to lose. It's been foreseen," Gargle gasped out as he tried to defend himself, but the light-trailing sword bit into his body. Smoke rose up each time Alex hit him with a sizzling sound like a welder cutting through thick metal. A burning sensation engulfed Alex's torso, as one clawed hand scored Alex's side. The pain cleared Alex's mind, even as it threatened to paralyze him. With a twisting of his wrist and a stretching of his arm, the sword wove around Gargle's arm stabbing deep into Gargle's thick neck.

Through the pain as if in slow motion, Alex noticed everything fading away. In his mind, he heard his subconscious say as if from a distance. *You've badly hurt Maleky. Now I should be able to fight him successfully.*

Another voice, a fading voice, guttural words said, "In here the Weird cheats for you, but—."

The sword was gone. *Who was I talking to?* Alex stood with Hymeron and Hheilea in the Weird with its white walls. A holo-field formed around Alex's torso and one arm. Over his torn and bloody torso, the field was pink. Overcome by his injury he started to slump toward the ground. Hheilea stepped close, slipping an arm around him.

"Can we get... out of here?" Alex asked, panting. And then he coughed and threw up all over Hheilea.

Hymeron backed away from them. "You two need to get cleaned up. And we can't leave until the holo-field heals your wounds. The Weird doesn't want to get in trouble for letting you leave wounded. In fact, you should see Gursha or there'll be a scar," Hymeron said. "What were you doing back there?"

"I, uh..." Alex paused and then said with more confidence, "I fought Gargle and killed him after his claws tore into me.... There was someone or something else."

As he spoke, the splattered liquid disappeared leaving only a faint smell of vomit.

Hheilea said, "After you drew your sword, you asked what's going on? Suddenly, you were fighting something we couldn't see. You weren't fighting Gargle. After Gargle attacked you from below, you fought him off. Next, you stopped, and said, but he warned me."

Alex shook his head. "My memory of it's confusing. It's like something was there, but I can't remember clearly. I drew my sword and then... Then Gargle attacked me from below. I fought him off and... charged him. I guess, I attacked kind of foolishly. Weldon would've been upset with me."

"What do you mean would've?" Hymeron asked. "He is upset."

"What?" Alex asked. "He wasn't there."

"He's an RE. Of course, he was watching," Hymeron said. "He and Gargle will probably talk about the fight."

Hheilea grasped Alex's arm. "We better get going. We're supposed to take you to Amable's office after we're done. Don't forget, my name is Hhy and I'm a boy. Never refer to me as Hheilea or as a girl."

Alex looked back at her. "Yes, Hheilea. I mean, Hhy."

Hheilea shook her head at him. "You're hopeless. Try not to do anything stupid."

She started to take a step, but tripped, pulling on Alex. He braced himself and kept her from falling, even as he felt overwhelmed, looking down into her violet eyes.

Alex grinned at her. "I'll try not to do anything clumsy either."

Hymeron tugged and yelled at both of them. "Come on! Stop your foolishness!"

Alex avoided looking at Hheilea and followed them out the same door they had come through months before. On the way to Amable's office, Alex put aside the mystery about Hheilea, and wondered what had been happening with everyone else. Ahead of him, Hymeron stopped and knocked at Amable's office. Alex looked around in surprise. *We're here already?*

The door opened, and Amable said, "Come in. Come in."

The three of them stepped through the doorway. Stick's voice, rising in near panic, greeted Alex. "What happened to you? Your shirt's all torn and bloody."

"Sorry. I didn't realize how bad it looks. The gaahr injured me at the end of my training."

Amable crowded past Hheilea to snatch Alex's hand and pumped it up and down. "Congratulations on facing a gaahr."

"You should've seen him," Hheilea said proudly. "He finished everything Gursha wanted him to do. The link he's developed with his AI is already better than what I can do. The AI itself is changing and growing to meet his demands."

Amable beamed. "Of course, he's quite the boy. He's going to do amazing things."

Alex stood still for a second, embarrassed by the praise. "Uh, yeah. I really wasn't that great." Changing the topic, he asked, "What's the rest of the flock doing now?"

"Today was their third day in the Hall of Flight," Amable answered.

Alex paused. *The time bubble. They don't know Twarbie told me about it. I already knew only a day had passed.* Feigning surprise, Alex said, "But, their first day was months ago."

Amable laughed. "You've a lot to learn, Alex. Only three days have passed for us. You and the kimley kids have been in a time bubble."

"A time..." Alex began and instead asked, "What should I do now?" *Three days? I thought it was one.*

"Your clothes are a great badge of courage, but get them changed and have a late lunch with the kimleys. Then come back here," Amable said.

Alex left. *I hope I fooled Amable with my act.* Momentarily he considered his mixed-up emotions about Twarbie and then another thought crowded in. *Why don't I remember all of the fight?*

Chapter Fifteen
T'Wasn't-To-be-Is

The three friends walked toward Amable's office after lunch. Hymeron snickered and said, "Hheilea told you the spicy, lillyputi dessert can be addictive."

Sweat ran down Alex's face. "I can't forget it. I need more." He stopped to sniff the air. Grasping his shirt, he jerked it to his mouthand sucked on a spot where the dessert had spilled, and sighed with pleasure.

Hheilea took Alex's arm and began urging him on toward Amable's office. At first, Alex let her, but after a couple of steps he slowed and looked back the way they had come. *What are they doing? The dessert's the other direction.*

She tugged at Alex's arm, but he refused to move. "I need your help, Hymeron. If we can get him to Amable's office, he can use *state of mind* to remove the addictive effects."

Alex leaned away from them, but step by step surrendered to their efforts. He pleaded, "Come on. Let me go back for seconds."

Hymeron tugged on Alex's hand. "That dessert needs to be placed on the restricted list for humans."

"Amable's office is just a few feet farther," Hheilea said.

The desire for the dessert continued to push against reality. *Who's talking? It doesn't matter. I must have more dessert.*

Hymeron kicked at the door, and it slid open.

Hheilea hung from Alex's hand, her feet dragging, as Alex began walking back the way they had come. "Amable, we need some help."

"I'm coming," Amable said.

Alex dragged her and Hymeron back down the passageway. From behind them came an amused Amable's voice. "What's going on?"

"Alex ate some lillyputi dessert," Hheilea said. "He's trying to go back."

Alex said, "I've got to have more."

Amable said, "It's my favorite dessert too."

Still getting dragged backward, Hheilea snapped, "Amable!"

"Yes, Hhy?" He laughed and said, "Just relax, Alex. We all love you. Everything's going to be fine."

Alex slowly stopped dragging the kimleys. Confused, he glanced down at them. "What just happened?"

"You had an addictive reaction to a dessert," Hymeron said. "Amable helped by calming you."

"What?" *Calming me? Dessert?* "I don't understand." Even as he spoke his mind cleared, and he remembered what Twarbie had said about Amable.

Amable gestured toward his office. "Come into my office. I'll explain."

Approaching the office, Alex began to hear a song playing. "Where's the music coming from?"

Once in the office, Amable pointed to a plant occupying one corner of the room. Its leaves were large, translucent, filled with liquid, and had fish-like creatures swimming in them.

Hheilea looked at the plant and asked, "Is it just starting to play the ode? I don't want to be here for it."

Amable brushed some dust off his clothes. "The Ode of Remembrance finished playing a little while ago. Now about what I did, you'll learn one of the effects from exposure to Dark Matter can be the ability to change the state of another creature's mind. The more you care for them, the better it works. I can encourage others around me to be at peace like I did for you."

Alex looked into Amable's large brown eyes. *Can he hypnotize me?* Huge bushy eyebrows waggled at him from over the eyes.

Chuckling, Amable said, "I suppose you're wondering if I can hypnotize you. The answer is no. There's a more enslaving way of affecting other people's minds. You'll learn about it in the Controlling Animals class."

Amable looked at each of them. Alex found himself shuffling his feet nervously. "Alex, earlier the boys gave me a glowing report about your training. Was there anything you would like to add? Did anything... out of the ordinary happen?"

Mind racing even as his mouth started to open to answer the question. *Does he know about Twarbie? How could he know about Twarbie? Maybe this is just about the fight.* "When I drew the sword to fight the gaahr, Hymeron and Hhei— say I started acting strange and fought something they couldn't see."

"Can you remember—?" Amable gave a sigh and opened a drawer in his desk. "Gursha wants to see you this evening. Work with her to figure out this mystery and give me a call if you need help. For now, take the afternoon off. The boys can show you around. Your flock leader, Ytell, will be in touch with you sometime today."

"How will I call you? I don't think my cell phone works here." Alex said. *I bet it's using my AI, like I did with the Weird.*

Amable paused his rummaging in the drawer to look at Alex and laugh. "Cell phone? Oh, that's a good joke. Contact me through your AI. If you want to talk to me, just think AI, I need to talk to Amable. Most of us have some form of AI. Stick's AI is how he interfaces with files and paperwork he's always working on. Everyone from Earth is receiving their own AI." Amable pulled a disc from the drawer. "Good, here it is. Hymeron, take this with you just in case Alex has a relapse of his addiction. Just aim the pointy end at him and push this button. He'll lose consciousness for a little while. It isn't dangerous, but make sure you don't play with it and bring it back tomorrow."

Hymeron took the small disc. "Great, this'll be fun. See ya."

Hheilea said, in an incredulous tone, "Do you really think it was a good idea to give him a stunner?"

Amable grinned in response. "Have you heard the saying, 'Give a man enough rope and he'll hang himself'? Consider this another test for you and your brother. If I hear any reports of people falling unconscious, I'll know who to blame and will have no qualms about restricting the two of you to your quarters. Besides, Alex really might have a relapse in the next few hours."

Hheilea scowled. "I wouldn't trust Hymeron with it. You should've given it to me. It's going to be your fault when he uses it. Come on, Alex, let's go."

"I'll be with you in a second," Alex said. "Amable?"

"Yes, my boy?"

"Did you know something strange is going on with me?"

Amable stepped forward and placed an arm around Alex's shoulder. "Weldon contacted me after you finished your training. He's favorably impressed by you and that's hard to do. And yes, he did tell me something strange happened. He thinks the string-sword might be a clue. He's going to try and see what he can find out."

"What—?" Alex started to ask.

"Now I know you have more questions, but I have many other responsibilities and I'm out of time for you. Work with Gursha. Talk to Weldon, and Ytell will help you all he can. Bye." Amable released Alex and pushed him toward the door.

The door opened and Alex jogged after the kimleys. "Sorry I took so long, let's go see my flock."

"You just want to see A'idah," Hymeron said with a grin.

"What?" Alex asked with an innocent expression, as he caught up. *I do like her, but she's young and then there's Twarbie and Hheilea. I need to forget about Twarbie.*

Hymeron elbowed him. "I saw you look all googly-eyed at her in the clinic."

Alex avoided looking at Hheilea. "No, not me. Well, maybe some at first. You know it's been very confusing for me. Okay, that was a lame excuse. You know she's much younger than I am. I think she's only twelve. I'm fifteen. What about you? How old are you?"

"I'm ten," Hymeron said and added, emphasizing the first three words, "and my brother is eleven. In the next five years, I'll make all the decisions for the start of my adult life."

Alex looked at Hymeron. "Really? You guys don't seem that young. Why would you make those decisions so young?"

Hheilea spoke quickly. "When we turn fifteen, we eventually start hearing a song. It's the beginning of our becoming adults. We're adults and almost always married before we're sixteen." Bitterly she added, "Then we lose touch with *now*."

"But why am I hearing—?" Alex started to ask, and then he said, "No way. I'd be getting married soon, and I'm way too young for that. What do you mean, losing touch with now?"

Hymeron said, "You need to meet our family. I'm warning you, for most people it's a crazy experience."

Alex walked along with them, stealing looks at Hheilea. Occasionally, he caught her looking at him. The song, crashing of waves on a distant shore and tinkling of wind chimes, mesmerized him. He almost laughed when Hheilea walked into a corner of the corridor. Then he did the same thing. He tried to regain control by looking away from her. Alex found himself wanting to run away. *What's going on? I really don't need getting mixed up with another alien.* Hymeron stopped at a normal looking door. *Would the family look like gypsies and maybe have crystal balls?*

Hymeron said, "We're here." A red haze settled over them and a voice asked, "Are you intending or planning any harm to this family?"

"No," both kimleys said and looked at Alex.

"No. I'm not," Alex said, truthfully.

The voice said as the door slid open. "You are cleared to enter, but an anomalous reading on Alex is noted in the records."

Alex paused at the door. He knew, just knew, entering this family's home was going to change him, and he wouldn't be able to go back. He stepped in, and his first impression was chaos. The colors of the walls changed as he watched. A stack of different sized bowls rested on the top of a green three-foot tall column. Other columns with stacks of things, and on the other side of the room three chairs surrounded a table. On a yellow column teetered a haphazard stack of stuff. At first glance he saw a spoon, many different colored threads, a rope, small bottles, and—. *That hair.* A man with multi-colored hair that shimmered, like butterfly wings as he moved, walked out of a hallway. He didn't look at them. Instead he looked back the way he came, yelling. "Hymeron, leave your sister alone!" Almost covered by the shoulder length hair, a green lizard stood on his shoulder looking at them with jewel-like eyes. The man turned back toward the doorway and shouted. "Don't do that!"

"Alex, meet my dad. Dad, this is Alex," Hymeron said.

"He was happy to meet you," the lizard on the man's shoulder said.

Alex held his hand out in greeting, but the man didn't look at Alex's hand. *His words don't make any sense.* "Why's he yelling at you two? You're not even where he's yelling."

"He's responding to some future, maybe not even one that will come to pass. Lately Dad has been worse than normal. It's like he overdosed on lillyputi dessert."

Their dad hurried to the bowls and grabbed one out of the middle of the stack, leaving the bowls above it hovering in the air. The hovering bowls slowly settled down onto those below. Meanwhile, he walked across the room and held the bowl at the edge of the table. The only thing on the table was a pile of beads on a pedestal. After a moment, he put the bowl back. The stack of bowls adjusted themselves to accept the bowl back into the stack.

"Over there's Mom," Hymeron said, pointing past a cluster of columns with their stacks.

Looking where Hymeron pointed, Alex saw a woman sitting quietly in a fourth chair. A small blue lizard scampered from her shoulder to place something in her mouth.

Alex raised his hand in greeting to the woman, but she just sat still, not looking at him. Hymeron walked into the room and slipped the bottom bowl off of the column.

"Why's she just sitting?" Alex asked Hheilea. "And what's up with the lizards?"

Hheilea turned a sad expression to Alex. "Mom shared too much of what she sees in the future. That made her view of the future so chaotic, she almost went catatonic. She's getting better.

"The lizards are cadleys. We all have them. When we're young, they come and go, but after our fourteenth birthday, they stay with us most of the time. It's a symbiotic relationship. We provide a safe place with food, and they help us with living in the now."

Hheilea moved her hair out of the way, and a bright green cadley scampered out of Hheilea's white hair. "Here, meet Neet. When I'm out in public, Neet has to stay hidden. We don't want anyone to know I'm fifteen, which would be at least eighteen in human years."

How old? Eighteen? Alex remembered a flash of green on Hheilea's bare back. "I think I might've glimpsed him once."

Neet tipped her head back and forth looking at Alex, and Hheilea said, "Neet's a girl. Hold your hand out."

On the other side of the room, Hymeron set the bowl on a chair below the edge of the table and sat down, resting his head on the table.

Alex held his hand out. Neet jumped onto it and scampered up to his shoulder.

Alex's eyes snapped wide open. He had heard a whispering in his mind.

Hheilea asked, "What?"

"I heard something in my mind. It was like a voice speaking to me from far away," Alex said.

Hheilea's expression changed to one of wonder and amazement. "You shouldn't have heard that. No one but a kimley can hear cadleys' telepathy, and their thoughts are heard by only a cadley's symbiotic partner or the mate of its partner. Neet asked me if she could taste your earwax. It's a delicacy for them."

The tinkling of wind chimes rising and falling like waves on a shore rose to a roar in his mind. Distracted by the music he just stood for a second before answering. "Yah, sure."

It was strange, feeling the cadley scamper up his neck. Alex grinned, as the cadley licked his ear. "She's tickling me."

Hheilea took Neet back. She looked intently at Alex and spoke firmly. "I've got to go to my room. Wait here."

The music faded in Alex's mind, as Hheilea walked away. He crossed the room to where Hymeron sat at the table.

Hymeron asked, "Where did Hheilea go?"

"She said she needed to go to her room," Alex said and then added cheerfully. "You were right, your parents are crazy, but your home feels good to me." And then more seriously he added. "Why did your mom share too much of the future?"

Hymeron took a deep breath. His voice grew sadder as he spoke. "We kimleys have a type of communication with our cadleys. No one understands how it works. Cadleys provide our adults with a link to reality or the now. Adults and their cadleys decide what needs to be shared with others. Mom and her cadley must've felt it worth the risk to her health."

"What was the information?" Alex asked.

Hymeron, with a limp hand, gestured at his mom and her lizard. "They informed Stick you needed to be one of the abductees. To my mom, you must be important. It's why we pulled so many pranks on you at first. I was kind of upset."

"I don't understand," Alex said, sitting down. "Your mom saw or sees something in the future that to her meant I needed to be here? So my very existence caused her problem?" *What do I say?* "How will I know what I'm supposed to do or how I'm supposed to be? I'll try to be... what?"

Alex held his face in his hands. "I'm sorry I caused your family so much trouble."

Hymeron placed a hand on Alex's shoulder. "I was an idiot. I don't know what Mom saw in your future, but if she thought it was important, we're going to help you, and besides we're friends. It isn't your fault. My mother made the decision. You must have an important part to play in the future."

Concern flooded Alex's voice. "But you don't know what it is I'm going to be involved in. How can you help me?"

"I don't know," Hymeron said and then he added with a big grin. "If only pranks had something to do with it. We're the best pranksters." A more serious expression took over. "You know we are good with computers. Also, I have lots of contacts. That might be a help. Maybe it has something to do with your training. At the end of your first year is a test. The six other groups of people Amable has gathered had to pass a test in their second year or their world was abandoned to its fate. I might be able to find out what the test is. Then we can help you pass the test one way or another."

"Thanks. That would be great," Alex said. "How do you handle all these problems with your life?"

"By going a bit wild as kids," Hymeron said chuckling and then added more seriously. "When we're adults, other species value our presence. Just like my mom's cadley sharing about you, the cadleys share some of what the adult is seeing of the future. Those glimpses of the future are very valuable." Hymeron finished with a scowl. "Remember what I said about Maleky? Others have been known to kill huge numbers of our race."

The news hit Alex like a physical blow. *That's terrible.* Falling back in his chair he knocked the pedestal over on the table. Beads spilled, rolling off the table. Scrambling to his feet and trying to catch them, he remembered the dad holding the bowl just where the beads were falling off. Now they landed in the bowl Hymeron had set up.

"Your dad knew I was going to knock over the pedestal. And how did you know to put the bowl there?"

"Yeah, he did. At times, it's very hard for them to separate the future they are seeing with their mind from what's happening now," Hymeron said. "From what we understand, their view of the future is very strange. To a certain extent, they can control how far into the future they are. Normally, he would've set the bowl to catch the beads like I did. Something about you seems to be disturbing him. I'm used to him and knew something like this might happen from his actions."

"How do you do anything with them?" Alex asked. "I mean they're here and yet they're not here."

"We get by. One of the things my parents do is just holding us. I guess that after enough time the future and present of the hug merge. They are very caring; it's hard for an outsider to understand," Hymeron said. In a more bitter tone he continued. "We have information about how life should be. In the pre-slavery days, the kimley communities had adults who

146

lived more in the now and they were very careful to stay there. Those adults took care of the children and much of the day-to-day routine.

"I don't understand," Alex said. "How can the future and present of a hug merge? It sounds a little like a Science Fiction story I read once. This guy traveled through time in a time machine. He wanted to meet someone, but kept jumping to the wrong time. Finally, he just waited for the person. But your dad's already here."

"That's it," Hymeron said. "Only Dad's subconsciousness is here. His consciousness is like that time machine you spoke of."

Alex looked at the kimley dad and shook his head in confusion. "I'm not sure I get it. What's your dad doing now?"

"It looks like he's securing things."

"What does that mean?"

"It's hard to say and it might be involved in something far in the future or a possible future not happening."

"Float" the lizard said.

"Okay, now you know more of why you don't understand my life," Hymeron said with a grin."

"Yeah, the more I know the less I understand," Alex said. *This is crazy, at least it can't get crazier.* A vision followed by dizziness made him reach out a hand to the wall. *What's going on? A purple bead? I'm showing Hymeron a purple bead, and he's telling me to put it back.*

"Are you okay?"

"Yeah, fine," Alex said, noticing a purple bead on the floor and picking it up. "Sorry, I just had a strange feeling about a purple bead," Alex said, showing Hymeron the one he picked up.

"Why did you pick that up?" Hymeron asked. "You should put it back with the rest."

"What?" Alex asked and began to hear familiar tinkling notes rising and falling like breakers on a coast. "Before I picked it up I saw you telling me to put it back." *That's a strange look Hymeron's giving me.*

Hymeron got a frantic look on his face. "This might be a T'wasn't-to-be-is vision. But that can't be. It doesn't happen to non-kimleys."

Alex responded without thinking, "What?"

Hymeron shook his head. "What a mess that would be. Hurry up. Let's get you out of here. Hheilea should be back out here. You go on out. I'm going to get Hheilea."

"Wha—?" Alex started to reply. With a surge of volume, the music, sounding as if from crystal wind chimes in a storm, stopped Alex in his tracks. Swaying to the crashing beats of the tinkling notes, he gazed across the room toward a hallway. A strange plant grew in an oval glass pot filled with water. At the base of the pot was the seed the plant grew from. The plant grew up in a circle, and its bloom dangled down to the bottom of the pot. *The seed the plant is growing from comes from its own flower. It can't be real.* As he gazed, flesh of a fruit rapidly started covering the seed.

Waving at the plant, Alex asked, "What's that?"

A panicked Hymeron answered, "Get out of here!"

Another question about the strange plant died on Alex's lips, as from the hallway came a figure dressed in a simple white gown. Hymeron ran at her and stopped, an expression of confusion covered his face, as he looked back and forth at Alex and Hheilea.

Hheilea... Mesmerized, Alex felt the music rhythmically pulling him toward her. Hheilea's delicate body stepped to the same beat. Her white hair gently moved a living frame to her elven face. His gaze locked on her startling violet eyes. Stepping toward her as she reached for him, their hands touched, and the world around him disappeared.

Chapter Sixteen
Scales

Blinking, Alex struggled to sit up, and then he lay back down as vertigo threatened his consciousness. Light-brown walls surrounded him and Hymeron stood back to the door glaring down at him. "What happened?"

Hymeron pointed down at Alex. "You idiot. You began to dance the T'wasn't-to-be-is dance with my sister. What do you remember?"

Irritation at Hymeron's words and aggressive tone cleared the fog in Alex's mind. "A figure coming toward me, it was Hheilea, and then... I don't remember any more. Where is she?"

"She's resting. She's an idiot too. What were you thinking? You shouldn't be dancing the T'wasn't-to-be-is dance with her."

"Get out of my face, Hymeron. Back off. I didn't dance it on purpose."

"Maybe you didn't you—, but the result would've been the same. I stopped it from happening. I used the device Amable gave me to knock the two of you out."

Alex struggled to get up. "You what?!"

Hymeron stepped closer, getting in the way of Alex getting up. "I knocked both of you out. I carried Hheilea back to her room, and I dragged you to this storage room. I was lucky no one saw me in the passageway."

Alex shoved against Hymeron's legs. *This fool stole something from me. The music and Hheilea are both wonderful.* "I tried to get you and Hheilea to explain about the music I was hearing during the last months, but you wouldn't. You kept ignoring me and saying I was imagining things. I knew Hheilea was hearing it too. How did it force me into the dance with Hheilea? What is this dance?" Other questions he didn't want to ask Hymeron filled his mind. *Where is Hheilea? I want to be with her. What's happening to me?*

In a calmer tone Hymeron began to explain. "The dance marks the beginning of two kimleys' transition to adulthood. We say the music is their future calling to them and bringing them together. Those who dance together..." Hymeron flushed and grew more upset as he said, "I don't know why or how you're caught up in this. It's wrong! You can't dance the T'wasn't-to-be-is."

Alex winced at the forcefulness of Hymeron's voice. "What does 'T'wasn't-to-be-is' mean?"

Hymeron leaned over Alex still glaring and breathing hard. He closed his eyes and began speaking from rote. "T'wasn't-to-be-is speaks of the adult life the kimley participants are moving into and uses a mix of tenses we are familiar with. Adults live in multiple possible futures. They experience the future in their present tense, but the thing is they can experience futures that probably can't happen. Those futures are called by my people, 'It-was-not-to-be' or 'T'wasn't-to-be'. Sometimes, the T'wasn't-to-be future ends up happening and therefore is. That future has become a T'wasn't-to-be-is. There's a legend among my people. It says our whole species is working to make a future a long time away, which is very much unlikely to happen, happen. It's called the 'T'wasn't-to-be-is Legend.' The term also refers to what you started to experience."

"Thanks. I understand better," Alex said. *How can they live in the future? What's it like? This is too much. If only I'd just gone back to my flock.*

"We need to get you back to your flock," Hymeron said, as Alex opened his mouth to ask another question. "Don't tell others about this and don't go looking for Hheilea."

Reluctant to follow Hymeron's orders, Alex began to stand up, when Hymeron pushed against his shoulder shoving him down.

"Stop," Hymeron said.

Alex froze clenching his hands, and growled, "Now what's wrong?" *I'm going to beat....*

Hymeron started rubbing at Alex's hair. Instead of angry, now his voice was frantic. "It won't come off."

"Stop that! What won't come off?"

Sitting back with a stunned expression, Hymeron looked into Alex's eyes, and tipped his head to the side. "See the iridescent scales on the skin of my temples?"

"Yeah. What about them?"

"When I start to become an adult, those scales move from my temples into my hair. I'll end up looking like my dad with iridescent colors shimmering as my hair moves."

At first, Alex didn't understand, then his mouth dropped open, and he frantically looked about the room hoping to find something he could see his hair in.

"It shouldn't be," Hymeron said. "The hair on your temples is starting to get the fine scales that will give your hair the color of my dad."

"No! Oh, no. I'm going to look like your dad?"

"My dad looks good."

Alex took a deep breath. He could really use Amable and his ability to calm others. He tried to calm himself to think of what to do, but his thoughts refused to be calm. Instead they picked up volume until they were screaming in his head. *This is too strange. I'm just a teenager and a human. I'm not an alien!*

Hymeron stood. "You have to stay here. I'm going to figure out a plan to deal with you."

"No!" Alex shot to his feet and shoved Hymeron against the wall. "You're not going to make any plans for me. I've had it with everyone and everything controlling me. I'm going to take care of this."

Hymeron stared back and Alex looked down to see Hymeron pulling the stunner out of his pocket. With one hand, Alex grabbed Hymeron by the throat and slammed him back against the wall. With the other, he struggled to tear the device from Hymeron's hand. Gasping and clawing with his free hand the kimley fought back, but Alex's months of training both with the kimleys and with Twarbie had endowed him with superior strength. It only took him a few moments to pull the disc from Hymeron. Remembering Amable's instructions, he pointed it at Hymeron and pushed the button. Instantly Hymeron collapsed.

Alex backed up against a wall and slid to the floor. *I'm free. Yeah, about as free as a moth in a spider web. How was I forced into the t'wasn't-to-be thing?* Alex tried not to think about Hheilea. *I can't be rational if I think of her.* Then his thoughts lurched to Twarbie and the time he'd spent with her. *I can't believe how I've grown to care for her. Forgetting her is about as impossible as forgetting to breathe.* The memory of their kisses burned in his mind and the music playing in his head died away. *It's not her choice to be terrible. Twarbie wants to be different. I want to help her, but she slammed the door on that possibility.* Alex ground his teeth at the memory of her warning. He heard her voice again and almost smelled her fragrance. "Don't try to find me or help me. Remember, if the other winkles know you're my friend, they'll force me to torture you to death. I can't stand that thought. Intsead, I'll just be how I'm expected to be."

He bashed his fist against the floor. Angry at how chance or fate had twisted his life into knots, he muttered to himself. "Twarbie might think she has no choice, but I do and I don't give up." He jumped to his feet and left the room. *But she told me,* 'You have fought back. I've had fun with you. Goodbye.' *She was just playing with me? Should I just forget about her? Can I?*

Slamming the door of the storage room behind him, he paused for only a second before thinking of Gursha. Alex hoped she could help him with his strange hair. After that, he would have to take things one step at a time. No matter what, he vowed, he would stay in control. Alex remembered what he'd told Peter. 'This is a chance for us to help other people.' *One thing I know, it won't be easy. I've got so many problems, and I'm just getting started.* The words of his father came to Alex. We *all need help with the little we have, to do what we can. I could use some help.*

As Alex walked to Gursha's clinic, the tinkling notes quietly rising and falling felt good and comforting. He knew

Hheilea heard the same song. His thoughts skirted the relationship he felt toward her. *It's like A'idah said, I feel like this strange-wonderful-experience with Hheilea has abducted me, but I'm too young for this, and I don't like its control over me.* He was still thinking of her as he reached the clinic.

"Hi, Gursha. Do you need to check how I'm doing?" Alex asked, entering Gursha's clinic.

A'idah lay in the middle of a blue haze, a medical holo-field, with a small amount of pink around her head. Her reddish-gold ringlets framed her face. A curved, very normal human ear showed on one side of her head. "Hi, A'idah. It's been so long since I've seen you. I missed you." The music grew very faint. *At last another human being, I can relax and be myself with. I don't need the drama those two alien girls brought into my life. I can trust A'idah and talk to her without worrying how she's going to react.*

Gursha pointed to a holo pattern on the floor. "Lie down over there. I would like to be sure there's no relapse."

"Hi, Alex. It's only been three days. I mean, I've missed you— Woah.... What happened to you? You're.... I mean.... Wow. How'd you get those muscles and you're tanned."

Gursha's voice interrupted. "A'idah, relax and lay back down. I need to finish your exam."

What do I tell her? The blue of the holo-field formed around Alex, as he leaned back and let it take his weight. His view of the room turned bluish and a little pinkish. "My training—."

"Ytell told the flock about your training. But how could you change so much in just three days? Who gave it to you? How did you get those muscles? ... You don't look sick anymore."

I can't tell her about Twarbie. "The kimley kids.... Well, actually something called the Weird," Alex said, relaxing as lights intermittently flashed by his eyes. "The crazy thing is..., it wasn't just three days for me. I've been gone for months. It was amazing, Now, I really like the kimley family."

A'idah sat up. Shock and something else echoed in her voice. "You were gone for months?"

Gursha pushed A'idah back down. "Hold on you two. I need to finish up with A'idah, and then you can talk while I'm checking out Alex."

He was grateful for Gursha's interruption. It would be easy to clear up the confusion about being gone for months, but what about the rest. *I can't tell A'idah about the alien ritual... or.... I need to just forget about Twarbie.*

In the background, Alex heard Gursha. "For a twelve-year-old, you're fine." And then she moved to him. "I'm ready for you, Alex."

A'idah stood, glaring down at him. "You've been gone for months and didn't talk to me."

"I was in something called a time bubble getting healthier in order to keep up with the flock. A'idah, you're the first friend I made here, and I wanted to have you and Zeghes give me the—."

"Then why would you spend all that time with the kimleys?" A'idah demanded.

"It wasn't my choice. Amable set it up with Gursha."

Gursha said, "He's telling the truth."

Relieved, Alex thought he was finally getting through to A'idah. A voice in Alex's mind spoke. |Alex, this is Hheilea.|

Alex's eyes opened wide and he blurted. "What?"

A'idah asked. "Who are you talking to?"

"Oh," Alex said. "I thought Gursha said something."

Again, Alex heard Hheilea in his mind. |Alex, I need to talk to you.| Hearing a chuckle in his mind made Alex smile. And then more words in his mind. |I just realized you might not understand what's going on. I'm using my AI and yours to talk to you. Just think to your AI and it will respond to me.|

Alex responded, |Hheilea?|

"Alex, what are you doing?" A'idah asked. "You're smiling and concentrating. It's as if someone or something else has your attention."

Gursha stopped what she was doing and crossed her four arms looking intently at Alex.

"I—" Alex started to say.

Gursha interrupted and stepped over to A'idah's side. "A'idah, I need you to leave and let me continue working with

Alex alone. He'll be free in time to go to his first class. I'll send him to your common room."

A'idah looked back and forth between Alex and Gursha. "Okay. I'll meet you in the common room. Then, you can tell me everything."

"Yes," Alex said, trying not to look too relieved as A'idah left. *She'll calm down and everything will be okay.*

Gursha sat down over another holo pattern in the floor and a blue haze rose up from the floor to support her in a comfortable looking, sitting position. With one hand, she touched the hair at her temple. "Alex, you need to talk to me. And don't worry about anyone coming in. I've set the clinic door on the privacy setting. No one will bother us. Except for..., I'm going to guess, Hheilea."

Meanwhile Hheilea had spoken to Alex. |Yes, that's it. Talking to me via your AI is just like talking, except without doing it out loud.|

Alex responded. |Give me a moment. I need to talk to Gursha.|

|Okay, I'll wait to hear from you. Just don't wait too long. It's important for us to talk.|

Lying on his back, with his head turned toward Gursha, Alex watched as she considered what to say. "Can I sit up?"

Gursha propped her head up with one arm. "No. I've found that lying down works better to enable speaking the truth. What happened before you got the new color at your temples?"

"You won't tell anyone?"

"I won't talk to anyone else about what you tell me, unless you specifically tell me to or if lives are in danger."

"What do you know about Hheilea?"

"I know her family has tried to keep her age a secret by having her wear a disguise and pretend to be a boy."

Alex gazed at Gursha's eyes considering her words even as he noticed another mark of her alienness. Just below her eyes he noticed a second small set of eyelids. Who could he really trust amongst these aliens? *It's all going to work out fine. I just need to stay calm.* "I was leaving the Soaley's home when

I started hearing music and then Hheilea appeared. We began the T'wasn't-to-be-is Dance."

Gursha's eyebrows lifted at that.

"Hymeron interfered by knocking us both unconscious."

Her eyebrows lifted higher.

"Hymeron had a device from Amable to use, if needed, to knock me out."

Her eyebrows lifted even higher.

"Amable gave a stunner to him because of an addictive reaction I had to a dessert. Afterwards, Hymeron dragged me to a storage room. When I came to I had...." Alex lifted his hand to his temple. He continued speaking, growing more and more frantic. "What's going on Gursha? Do you have a mirror? Hymeron's really upset. Hheilea wants to talk to me and I feel a strange connection to her. A'idah likes me. She's human even though she's a lot younger than me. I haven't met anyone like her. I need her friendship. It's not just that she's really cute. We have so much in common, but if she knew about what's going on with Hheilea.... She'd be upset." *And then there's Twarbie. What am I going to do? Calm, I've got to calm down and be like the British spy, cool and always in control.*

Gursha reached into the holo-field and held Alex's hand. He squeezed her hand in response. He continued in a calmer voice. "I don't want to upset A'idah. Hheilea and Hymeron have become my friends, but now Hymeron's upset. I'm upset. I've been abducted and told my whole world is in danger."

Gursha held a hand up. "I know you're having a hard time. Let's start with A'idah. You shouldn't tell her about the T'wasn't-to-be-is Dance and Hheilea, not now. A'idah has too much to deal with herself. You need to treat her carefully. She's looking to you and Zeghes for stability in this situation, but there is someone else she could turn to and I don't think he'd be as good for her as you."

Alex nodded his head. *I know how my folks would want me to treat her, and she's so young.* Alex grinned at Gursha. "I need her for stability too. Wait. You said there's someone else she could turn to?"

"Don't worry about him," Gursha said. "Also, Hymeron will get over being upset. This situation with you and Hheilea is just as strange for them. Now about the dance and your hair, I think that psychedelic color with your dark hair is going to look great."

"Gursha," Alex said, feeling appalled at her thought. While the one word, 'him' echoed in his mind.

"Just joking. I think I can do something about the color. No one will notice it now. Give me a second, and I can also get rid of the scars from your fight with the Gaahr."

Alex lifted his arm up. "I want to keep the scar on this arm. There's so much of the fight I don't remember." *Who would A'idah turn to for stability?*

The holo-field holding Alex lifted him up to his feet and he stood. "When do you want me to come back?"

"I'll send you an AI message. Now go on. The first class is interesting. Enjoy it and try to unwind. Remember your teacher is an alien and might be a bit revolting or strange to you."

Alex couldn't imagine being able to relax as he hurried toward the common room. *I want to scream.* His problems were just too much for him to comprehend or deal with. The peaceful rising and ebbing of *Hheilea's music* slowly captured his attention, and he realized Gursha hadn't said what to do about Hheilea.

Alex stopped. Carefully he thought to his AI, |Hheilea?|

The sweet voice of Hheilea rushed through his mind. |How did it go with Gursha? You can't come. Our dance would restart and I promised Hymeron we would wait, at least for a few days. He's having a serious meltdown, until he calms down we need to wait. I'm so happy to be able to talk to you. I was very upset about how young you are, but now I'm at peace with it. Since I'm more mature, I—|

In desperation to stop the flow of words, even as a warm glow of contentment flooded his heart, Alex thought one word. |Wait.|

A repentant, |I'm sorry.| came back.

I can't do this. |We need to understand what's happening.|

|I do understand. It's the 'T'wasn't-to-be-is' Dance. We are meant to be together. I'm so happy.|

Cautiously, Alex responded. |I'm human.|

|Tears.|

How can I hear the thought of tears? |Hheilea? Are you okay?|

|Sniffles. I.... I'm okay, just a bit confused. This is supposed to be a very happy time for both of us, but.... Are you sure you're human?|

|You've seen my temples. I don't have the scales on them.| *BUT WHAT ABOUT THE SCALES I'M GETTING IN MY HAIR?* |Hheilea, talking with you makes me very happy. We'll figure this out. Right now, I need to go to my first class.|

|Thanks, Alex. I'll get you some information about our new life. I mean the life we'll have after we finish the T'wasn't-to-be-is. I trust you. Talk to me soon. Please. Good bye.|

|Bye.| *My-Our new life?* Alex needed to scream, but instead he started running toward the common room. Two thoughts battled in his mind for attention. What boy could A'idah turn to? And what was he going to do about Hheilea and Twarbie? He ran harder trying to push away the thoughts, worries, and a sickening sense of horrible trouble. *Something really bad's about to happen. It can't be the T'wasn't-to-be-is. That was wonderful. Except crazy. I wonder what it is, this time.*

Chapter Seventeen
Lepercauls Eat

Racing around a corner, Alex ran straight into a misty green cloud. He responded to the strange tingling on his skin with a gasp, only to feel tingling in his mouth. Coughing and choking, Alex stumbled out of the cloud.

"Way to get friendly," cloud girl said, with a chuckle. As Alex recovered from his coughing fit, she oozed through the air at him.

Alex looked up at her. "Sorry for running into you and thanks for helping me with the baby lepercaul the other day."

The cloud girl came to a stop. "Your months of training in the Weird really have made a big difference. You're no longer nervous about me."

Alex said, "Wha—?"

But the cloud girl kept talking. "Others are starting to complain about the resources diverted for your special training, but I think it might be worth it. There's something about you. And I'm not just talking about all the stories of the kimley's interest in—."

Her words slammed aside Alex's thoughts of hurrying to his class. He held up a hand. "Wait. How did you know about my training?" *And what does she know about the kimleys?*

"You Earthlings have so much to learn. It's really too bad you're only getting a year. If there were the resources to put all of you into a huge time bubble, then maybe Earth would have a chance. I knew about your training because of the ship. Anyone can talk to it, but it isn't always very helpful. Fortunately, this deem ship does obey Amable and his team, but it still likes to keep secrets, and it is devious. The ship didn't know what happened in the Weird room, but it knew

159

about the time bubble being setup around the Weird and the room. It had to know because of the interface troubles created between the Weird's computer and other computers external to the time bubble. Sorry for rattling on. I'm kinda upset about today's news."

Then she shouldn't know about Twarbie, but would everyone know about the T'wasn't-to-be-is? I'm going to be late for class, but I've got to know about this. "What are the stories about the kimley's interest in me?"

"Mostly rumors. The one thing which started them is Mrs Soaley caused your abduction. Everyone knows the kimley's danger in sharing information from the future. I heard she almost died. I wish I could get an invite to her home. I've heard the craziest stories."

It sounds like she might not know about the T'wasn't-to-be-is "The ship doesn't share information about their home?"

"No, everyone's homes are private. Well, I should be going. It was great meeting you again."

"Okay." *Today's news.* "Wait a second. Earlier you mentioned today's news making you upset. What's going on?"

"The winkles are having a ceremony. Ever since the winkle mutiny happened any ceremony of theirs puts everyone on edge."

Twarbie stuff. I am going to forget about her. "Oh, thanks for the information." Alex was going to add, I better get to class and let you go, but the cloud girl, after a short pause, kept talking.

"You'll be happy to hear the winkle girl, who bit you, is in big trouble. I wouldn't want to see what happens to her. The winkles are terrible."

With a frozen heart, Alex managed to gasp out a question. "Where's the ceremony?"

"Amable reserved the Hall of Flight for them," She said with a snort. "I guess it's all part of his gentler, kinder program. He's..."

Alex didn't hear the last of what she said. He was running. "Ship, what's the quickest route to the Hall of Flight?"

"Do you want a guide?" The ship's voice said in a strange tone.

"Yes, of course."

"Okay. Have fun."

A ball of light materialized in front of Alex and he ran following the bouncing guide. *Will I be in time? What can I do?* Digging deeper, he pushed to go faster. *Have fun? Why did the ship reply so strangely? Almost as if it knew a joke it was keeping secret. It almost sounded evil.* "Ship, is something dangerous or unusual about this path?"

"Oh..., it's just that the shortest route goes through the lepercaul wild. Any other path is much longer. She's still alive, for now." And then it laughed.

Alex remembered Twarbie's words, I didn't want to attempt going all the way through the wild with just salt for defense. Sweat began to bead-up on his forehead. *Too bad I'm not sweatier. Maybe the salt of my sweat would keep the babies at bay.* Coming around a corner he bounced off a wall and ahead Earthlings walked toward him filling the hall. He yelled, "Make a hole!"

Whether or not the humans and other Earthlings understood the meaning of the phrase, they did understand his purpose. As Alex raced toward them, humans and animals crowded against the two walls. In front of him an alligator dropped to the floor. With two running steps across the alligator he passed through the crowd. "Sorry."

Alex ran around another corner and dodged an alien. *How long does Twarbie have? What are they doing to her?* Sweat burned in his eyes. Alex swiped at his forehead with a hand. His sweaty shirt stuck against his skin. At last he came to a long passageway with massive double doors at the end. Skidding and stumbling to a halt, he gasped out. "Ship..., open the... salt chamber."

A doorway appeared in the featureless wall to his right. Alex ducked through it. A large barrel of salt stood in one corner of the closet. He paused looking at it. *What can I do? There aren't any bags. It would be suicide to go through this wild even if I had something to carry it in.* Alex thrust his hands into the salt. It stuck to his sweaty skin. In seconds, Alex stripped and began rubbing the salt over his body. *I'm taking too long. Snatching his clothes off the ground he dressed.*

When he grabbed his shirt he paused. Then he jammed it into the barrel. In seconds he filled it with salt. Whirling about he raced to the big double doors.

The ship asked, in a slightly amazed voice. "Do you really want to go into the lepercaul wild?"

"Yes. I'm going through it."

The big doors opened. "We'll see how far you get. I'm informing Amable about your stupidity. He gets upset if students commit suicide."

Alex looked into the area beyond the doorway. In the dim light, he could only get a vague sense of the room. *This is crazy. She needs me.* He stepped into the wild.

Amable's voice sounded in his mind. |Alex, don't stay in the wild. Go back. What you're attempting is suicide.|

A cloud of fog swirled across uneven ground toward him. It flowed past rough protrusions sticking a foot or two up from the ground.

|I'm going to the other side.|

Something, a cloud of stuff puffed up from one of the protrusions. With high pitched noises, the cloud surged up the rough sides grabbing at the particles.

It's not fog.

|Alex, you're just a teenager still learning how to fit in. You don't know the danger of the lepercaul wild, much less ready to face it and survive. No one can save you. Please don't die.|

Alex ignored Amable's pleadings. *I don't need distractions.* Part of the cloud peeled away from that feeding and flowed toward Alex. *I can make it through here.* Something larger moved in the gloom. Fear trickled down his spine. He tried to move faster, but the uneven ground and dim lighting slowed him. *I don't want to stumble on a big baby.* Thumping sounds came from an uncertain direction. Some of the cloud reached his shoes. Now Alex could make out baby voices from the high pitched noise.

"Ow. He hurts me."

"Ow."

"Bad, bad."

"Winkle?"

"Run."

The cloud pulled back from his feet. Alex could make out separate-indistinct-stubby-babyish shapes. It was a crowd of very small baby lepercauls. Out of the gloom a waist high baby thumped, lurching toward Alex. The lepercaul stomped on some of the distracted tiny babies. In one of its feet Alex could see struggling little bodies. *It's eating them. What a terrible way to die.* The bigger baby's other foot showed why it lurched. That foot was very small.

The odd looking baby said, in its very babyish voice, "Don't salt me again. Please. I'll do what you want."

The germ of an idea started to grow in Alex's mind. "What happened to your foot?"

"I ran from a winkle. It threw salt at me. Some hit my foot."

"Follow me."

"Okay."

Alex continued on, following the bouncing light deeper into the gloom. *Where's the other door? Familiar thumping sounds whipped Alex around.*

Two more waist high babies charged at him. They argued as they ran.

"I saw the food first."

"Me eat."

Alex shifted the shirt of salt. It was getting lighter. It's leaking. He thrust a hand into the salt and lifted it up. Fear screamed in his mind threatening to paralyze him. "Stop or I'll salt you."

The babies thumped to a stop. "Okay. We'll eat you when you run out of salt."

"Follow me if you don't want to get salted."

"Of course we follow you. You'll make big meal for many of us, like him." The baby talking pointed behind Alex.

Alex jumped sideways and looked back. Behind him, a giant baby slowly approached. *Two of me would fit inside him with lots of room to spare.* An involuntary shiver of fear ran down his spine. Alex waved his fist threateningly and flung a few grains of salt. "Stay back or I'll salt you."

In a voice not so babyish, it said. "No problem, I'm ready to become an adult."

163

Keeping an eye on the three smaller ones, Alex tried to slowly follow his guide. "You won't be able to eat me if I salt you."

A voice, after a second Alex recognized it as Hheilea's, spoke in Alex's head. |Alex, what are you doing?|

"True but I'll get a bit of you and then others will finish eating you. I hate you winkles. Be nice to have one die." The giant swung an arm at Alex.

An insistent Hheilea distracted him. |Alex, answer me.|

He ducked to the side almost too slow. |Leave me alone. I'm trying to stay alive.|

The giant baby swung another arm. Alex considered using his salt, but thought—.

Hheilea's furious voice interrupted. |Don't you dare die.|

|If you don't leave me alone, I will.| He tried to think through the fear and distraction. *What am I going to do?*

"Why don't you just throw your salt at me?" The giant asked. Now it reached out with both arms moving faster.

More thumping sounds came from the direction Alex needed to go. He stopped and in desperation blurted out. "I'm not a winkle. I hate winkles."

"I hate them more. They forced me to do things."

The thumping grew louder. A quick glance revealed a group of large babies charging him. Alex said to the giant, "I'm going to attack winkles. They will get eaten."

The big babies were too close. Alex lifted his shirt to throw the salt.

"Wait!" Thundered the giant.

The babies slammed their legs in one final step and stopped. Alex, heart pounding almost out of his chest, held the shirt as it slowly dribbled salt. In terror, he looked at the gathered horde of lepercauls. *I've gotta stay calm. I'm the British spy. Why am I doing this? Twarbie.* "You can eat the winkles too, if you hurry."

"But we can't leave here."

"Follow me. I'll open the doors for you. Then I'll take you to them."

"Won't they salt us?"

"They only have salt when they come in here to torture you."

Two of the big ones moved to attack Alex.

"I'm hungry."

"Me too, we not wait for this idea."

Alex swung his shirt back to heave the salt at them. He didn't worry about the salt spilling out. There wouldn't be enough salt anyway. Amable had been right.

"Stop!" A voice bellowed from over Alex's head.

The big babies stopped again. In relief, Alex looked up. The giant towered over him. *If it falls on me, I'll die a horrible death feeling myself getting digested.* The relief turned back to terror. *No. I won't be able to save Twarbie. I'm dead.*

The voice above Alex boomed out again. "Anyone of you, who takes the smallest bite of this... helper, will get eaten by me. Helper's too salty to properly enjoy anyway." The baby tipped forward to look down at Alex. "How will we be able to stop the winkles from controlling us?"

Alex tried to organize his thoughts, but terror kept wiping away ideas. Finally, he just went with the truth. "The winkles are very good at something called 'Controlling Animals.' The defense against it is love."

"What is love?"

"It's caring for others."

"When I was very small all of us little ones cared for each other, otherwise we got eaten. Eventually, the biggest starts to eat the rest, no more care then. Why should I care? The parents teach us to not care."

I'm running out of time with this useless conversation. I've got to be calm. If I don't convince this giant, I'm probably doomed. Just keep it simple. "Just like when you were small, friends watch out for each other. Having someone who cares for you is a good thing. You feel good from their care."

"Okay. Lead us to the winkles." In a quiet voice he added. "If you don't take us to the winkles I'll eat you first, but I'd rather not. I think I want to talk more with you."

Alex gulped, nodded, and slowly began to follow the guide as the babies all shuffled out of his way. The giant baby stayed terribly close to Alex.

When the last baby moved out of the way, Alex walked faster and then slowly began to run. Behind him, the thumping increased in volume until it sounded like a stampede of babies. In the light of the guide Alex spotted another double door. They opened for him and stayed open, as he stood in the doorway.

The giant thumped up sending chills down Alex's back. "Lepercaul babies we'll have fun, but mind me and Helper or you'll regret your mistake, until I eat you. No one tastes our helper as you go by. Just stand in the hall and wait until we lead you again."

"Stop snacking." He added as a bigger baby leaned down, plunged a hand into a smaller one, and started sucking it up. "You'll ruin your appetites. Wait for the winkle meal."

With, "But I'm hungry." the baby pulled its hand out of the deflated lepercaul.

The little one wobbled away, meanwhile the other babies of the horde filed past Alex. Some of the largest paused to look at him, but after looking up over Alex's head they all entered the hall. There they chattered with and poked at each other.

"We're outside."

"Hungry."

"Where's the food?"

"Don't poke me."

"When are we going to eat?"

"When do we get there?"

The giant said, "We better get them moving before they stop nibbling, and start eating each other." And then he added to the other babies. "Stop nibbling on each other."

Alex said, "Good idea. You lead them. Just follow the bouncing ball. I'll stay in the back of our horde and watch out for stragglers." *At least Hheilea stopped pestering me, but now she's probably mad.*

"Okay. Just don't let one of the stragglers eat you. I want to talk with you after we eat the winkles."

All of the baby lepercauls stared at Alex, as the giant thudded past them.

166

Yeah, not getting eaten seems like a good idea. This is crazy. "We need to hurry before the winkles find out you are coming for them. We don't want them to run away."

With shouts and a thundering roar the horde of babies crowded after the giant. None looked back at Alex. The bigger ones forged toward the front while the smaller fell behind. Soon, Alex could no longer see any of the biggest and then even the sounds died away to just the quieter steps of the smaller babies.

Amable's voice sounded in his head, |Alex, you made it. Amazing. The ship is telling me a crazy story about you and Lepercaul babies. What are you doing?|

|I'm going to save Twarbie.|

|How? What's your plan?|

Alex ran around a corner to find the small babies milling about in the hall. Their voices were raised, some in hunger, some in pain, some mad, and a couple from the closest were very threatening.

"I'm hungry."

"Where did the leaders go?"

"Stop eating me. I'm going to tell on you. The giant said 'No snacking.'"

"Oooh, it's the not-a-winkle. Let's eat him."

"Eat him."

Alex skidded to a halt. He held up a shirt with very little salt left in it. "Stay back." |I'm going to use the babies to distract the winkles and then I'll save Twarbie.| *I've got to get them moving again, before they—.*

|Okay, I'm redirecting your big babies to a floor level entrance.|

A new bouncing ball appeared in the midst of the babies. The two closest to Alex stepped toward him. "You can't stop us both with the little salt you have left."

Chapter Eighteen
Dying

|The guide I sent you will lead to a balcony over the winkles. The small babies can jump from there. They'll bounce.|

Not waiting for the rest of Amable's words, Alex charged the two approaching babies, swinging his shirt and yelling at the top of his voice, "Out of my way! I'm following that light to food, lots of food!"

At first the milling babies all reacted to Alex's yelling by backing away or even starting to run from him. In front of everyone the ball of light took off bouncing through the air. Once Alex ran in amongst them, the lepercauls all reacted by joining with Alex in racing after the ball. Around him, babies shouted.

"Don't yell at us! We'll be good!"

"Food!"

"Eat. Time to eat!"

The two babies considering eating Alex backed out of his way and he sprinted past them. Behind him he heard their voices and the thumping sounds of running.

"Slow down. We want food."

"Yes. Wait."

Alex wasn't sure if they spoke of the food he had shouted about or if they were speaking of him. *I've just got to keep moving.*

|The babies should provide the distraction you want. Good luck with your plan. Also, I'm clearing everyone out of the babies' way. Fortunately, the babies you released haven't injured anyone.|

The light swung around a corner and the babies tumbled into a struggling mass as they tried to make the turn without slowing down. Alex slammed painfully against the wall as he avoided the baby pile-up. He shoved off the wall and took a stride after the light, but then he paused looking back. *What's my plan? I need these babies to distract the winkles. I've got to get them going. Yelling seemed to bother them.*

Behind Alex the last two babies jumped onto the pile. Muffled voices rose from the struggling mass.

"Get off."

"Stop eating me."

"I'm going to tell the giant."

"Giant not here."

"This fun."

"Don't bite me. I'll bite you back."

Alex could hear other voices too muffled to understand as he hurried back. Then he screamed at them. "The giant is coming and he's going to be mad at you!"

The pile shook, and with crying and whining the outer layers began to peel off.

"Not my fault."

"He did it first."

"I wasn't doing anything bad."

"He did it, not me."

A smaller baby struggled to its feet and took a few wobbly steps away from the diminishing pile. *Wow it's weak. It probably can hardly eat at all in this state.* With that thought a real plan blossomed in Alex's mind. Rushing forward he scooped the weak baby from the ground. Instantly, needles of pain began nibbling at him. He tried to ignore the pain telling himself a lie. *It isn't any worse than a mosquito bite or two or three or four.* Alex turned and started after the ball of light. In response, the ball of light resumed bouncing through the air.

Alex called back to the other babies. "We're going to go eat some winkles. All of you can stay here and wait for the giant."

A chorus of voices rose from behind him.

"Baby's nibbling on him."

"Helper's letting baby."

"I nibble too."

"Eat."

"We eat too."

"Eat."

Through the pain of his hands, Alex heard the babyish voices talking about eating him. In response, he picked up his pace. The voices behind him faded. A high-pitched laugh, born of pain-terror-and the craziness of baby voices sounding so dangerous, gasped from between his lips. Ahead, he recognized an entrance to the Hall of Flight. *This is too crazy. I've got to keep it together. I can be cool, just like—.*

Hheilea's voice spoke again, with consternation pounding in every word. |Alex, what's happening to you?|

|I'm fine.| Alex lied. He had to. She couldn't handle the truth. Alex stumbled and almost fell. A heavy weight hung from his arms. Behind him, he could hear the voices growing louder.

"Slow down."

"We're hungry."

Hheilea's words resounded with anguish. |You're not fine. I can feel your pain. I'm coming to you.|

|No. Don't. It's too dangerous. How can you feel my pain?|

Alex staggered through the doorway onto a balcony. He could hear screaming in the distance. Tripping, he fell toward the edge.

Hheilea responded, as Alex struggled to stand and not tumble off the balcony. This time he briefly felt some humor mixed with her concern. |Silly, we're almost one. Of course, we can feel each other's feelings. There's so much you need to learn about our future. Whatever you're doing stop it!|

Almost one? Our future? She knows my feelings? I can feel hers? At the last question, a door opened and Alex could feel Hheilea's concern for him and—. Alex squashed the feelings. *I'm not ready for this. It feels wrong to know her feelings. I don't want her knowing how I feel.*

|It's okay, Alex. You're just a boy-a teenager. I understand. I'll be there to help soon.| He could feel Hheilea's tears running down her face. |Don't you dare die.|

Alex lurched away from the edge. For a long second he stared at a bubble circle next to him. The screaming.... *Twarbie!* His heart ached and he staggered into the circle. The familiar tingling started immediately.

Fury mixed with more anguish poured from Hheilea. |How can you feel that way for someone else! That's wrong! I don't understand. You've started the T'wasn't-to-be-is with me! Was she in the Weird?|

Alex didn't know what to say. He could hear the babies running at him. *I can't go until this bubble finishes growing. Will they attack me? Does it matter? I don't think I'm going to make it.*

"You're nice."

Confused, Alex looked around.

"I'm stronger. Thanks for helping me."

Alex looked down. He no longer held the baby. At some point, it had grasped his arms and now hung from them. It had filled out with a murky red substance. A wave of dizziness struck him as he looked back at the on-rushing horde of babies. He leaned against the bubble wall, trying not to faint.

The small baby said, "Are you okay? I stopped nibbling. You saved my life."

Other babies thudded against the wall of the bubble trying to get to Alex.

"Eat."

"Eat."

"Eat."

Breathing deep, Alex gathered his strength. *I've got to do this. He said to the horde,* "You can't get through the bubble. Your food is below. Jump off and nibble on the winkles below."

"I not nibble. I eat."

"Food."

"Winkles not hurt us?"

"We eat them."

A few more questions and confident statements about eating winkles and then the horde ran over the edge. Alex sighed and slumped farther down into the bubble. Maybe the babies would cause enough trouble to save Twarbie without him. His eyelids were so heavy.

"How come little baby no longer eating or even nibbling on you?"

Alex looked and there were the two bigger babies, which had kept threatening to eat him. "Jump off and go eat the winkles." There was a problem with telling them to do that without him, but trying to think took too much effort.

"He saved my life. I don't understand, but I don't want him to die. I might not have stopped nibbling in time. Helper is very weak."

The two babies stood with their hands toward him. Alex grinned at it, even as the view seemed to be growing dim. *It's getting dark in here. What are they doing?*

One of the big babies said, "He cared for you... and now you care for him. I don't understand."

Alex barely made out what the other one said, "What is this feeling? I don't remember this feeling."

Was Hheilea screaming at him? Alex couldn't make out her thoughts-words, but the feelings... The sounds around him faded. Out of the descending darkness blossomed a bright light. Warmth enveloped his body. *This must be the end.* The darkness receded, leaving him in confusion looking at the two babies standing in front of him. A glow faded from their hands and their faces registered shock.

One stammered a question. "Are... are... you okay?"

"Yes," Alex said without thinking. It was true. He felt fine. "I've got to go save someone. I'll talk to you guys later." His bubble dove over the edge. Behind him, he heard the babies responding, until distance made them impossible to hear.

"We'll help. Not want—."

Below him chaos reigned. From the other side of the vast hall came shrieks punctuating the arrival of the giant and the big babies. Winkles ran in every direction trying to avoid the bouncing babies. Alex spotted a group of winkles standing still around a platform and writhing on the platform –Twarbie-. Alex leaned forward in his bubble, urging it to drop faster. Alex spoke to the baby still hanging from his arms, with a voice filled with urgency. "When we get down there, I'll need you to nibble on me and on the winkle I set you on, but—."

In a plaintive tone it said, "I don't want to nibble on you or anyone else. I might kill them, and it hurts others even if I'm just nibbling."

What's happened to this creature? Alex snapped the words out. "Look, if you don't nibble on me, the winkles might kill me. I'm trying to save the winkle being tortured. Just go along with my plans. See the winkle holding a knife? She's going to kill the girl on the platform and me if we don't fool them all."

"Okay. I'll help. Can she stop screaming?"

A bouncing baby glanced off the bubble and Alex fell to the floor. *That's right the little guys don't like screaming.* "The big babies aren't bothered by the screaming. You can do this. Remember if you fail, I and the winkle girl die."

The baby started to reply. "I—." They reached the ground and Alex hadn't slowed the bubble enough. Coming in at an angle, they rolled knocking down the winkles gathered by the altar. The bubble dissipated and Alex slammed against the altar. He jumped to his feet, and with the baby clutched in his hands turned to the winkles. Not waiting for them to take charge of the situation, Alex swung the baby at their faces. "You wimps! You don't have any spines. You torture others, but when it comes to your own you can't do a very good job of it. I'll show you how to torture an enemy. I'm getting even with her for what she did to me." *Okay now to torture Twarbie, but then what? Can I really do this to her?*

One of the winkles jumped to her feet. "You're crazy. Don't you feel the baby eating you?"

The words made Alex aware of the pain. *It doesn't have to eat quite that vigorously.* Alex shook the baby at them. "See. This is another example of how weak winkles are. I bet you couldn't hold this baby without screaming."

The winkle stepped closer to Alex. She looked like Twarbie. "Ha. You don't know how strong I am. And by torturing Twarbie you're actually proving what she told us. She said 'I had fun playing with the human boy's emotions. Right until the end of my time in the Weird, he thought I was telling him the truth. All the time, I kept coming up with new ways of torturing him.'"

Through the pain, Alex almost grinned at those words. At the same time doubt tore at his heart. *Is it the truth?* It didn't matter, he would save Twarbie. Hot tears streamed down his cheeks. The battle in his heart at hurting Hheilea fed them. His agony at Twarbie no longer screaming, but keening, a low wailing sound ripped sobs from him. His frustration at his lack of control concerning the girls gave him anger. He screamed at them through the tears. "She was terrible!" *What am I going to do?*

An old crone with a knife stepped forward. In a hoarse, evil voice she said, "Then take this knife and kill her."

Ignoring her weapon, Alex stepped closer and she shrank back from the baby. He used his disgust at the winkles and let it flow in his response. "And give her a quick end? Bah. I want her to suffer like I did." *I can't stand having Twarbie in such agony.*

"Lookout, Helper!"

"Huh." Alex looked up and dodged to the side as a baby fell. A scream signaled why it didn't bounce away. Then the scream was cut off. The small baby had grabbed the winkle by her face. The winkle flung her knife. Spinning through the air it just missed Alex. She tried to tear the lepercaul from what was left of her face. In the struggle, she fell to the ground. A voice ragged with pain and urgency tore his attention away.

"Quickly, take my daughter out of here. The winkle, which looked like Twarbie, had a medium-sized baby wrapped around her legs, but the woman ignored it, pointing at Twarbie. Get her out of here."

Alex turned to obey. But a familiar voice distracted him.

"Stop eating her face. Watch me. This is more fun and feels better."

A bright light shined from behind him. Alex looked back to see one of the babies holding his hands out at the old winkle. She stood to her feet, and felt her healed face. In an amazed voice, she said, "You healed me. How? And why?"

Another baby's voice spoke from behind him and Alex slowly turned, feeling as if he was caught in a time bubble.

"This one looks terribly hurt already. I guess I'll put her out of her misery."

The giant baby jumped onto the altar and landed on top of Twarbie. The wailing stopped. His skin seemed to ooze around her taking her whole body inside of him. Red fluid began clouding the translucent giant's body.

"NO!" Alex dropped the baby and started forward. He only thought of jumping on the giant, trying to claw her out of the baby. The knife lay in front of him. He snatched it up and demanding his AI to help him make the jump, leapt for the giant's back. He wasn't going to make it. Twarbie's form disappeared from view in the murky red fluid surrounding her. Then a boost from a gravity generator slammed into him. Just before he rammed the giant, Alex slashed at it with his knife and dove into the cut.

-Pain-. *Keep my mouth and eyes shut*. His searching hand found Twarbie. *-Pain-*. Darkness threatened to descend on him for the second time that day. *Got to... get her... out*. He kicked against something with his feet. *Pull her. She's got to live*. With his knife hand he slashed. Sanity destroying agony tore at him. *Shove her... shove her out*. Then her body moved and Alex let the pain stealing darkness take him. But this time, light didn't fight off the night.

Chapter Nineteen
Funny

"He should be coming around."

What? ... Where am I?

"Hello, Alex."

That's... Someone's holding my hand. Strange colors shifted just above him. He blinked. Lime-green and violet hair waved. *What?* Alex tried to lift a hand, but his arm felt leaden and didn't want to move, so instead he blinked again. Amable's face with his large, golden eyes gazed at him. Alex stared for a long moment and then like a tide, his memories rushed in. "Twarbie! She was getting eaten!"

Amable patted Alex's hand. "Calm down or Gursha will toss me out."

"But, sir. What happened to her?"

"I see you must know. Among the many things you did last week, you saved Twarbie's life. I hear she's very mad at you."

Alex grinned in relief. *The pain had been worth it.* "I hope she's mad." At Amable's puzzled expression, Alex added, "I mean she wouldn't be the Twarbie I hope she is if she wasn't mad."

Amable raised a bushy eyebrow. "I suppose that makes sense to you."

I shouldn't let her secret out. "I meant..., you know all the winkles are quite mad. I hope she suffers."

Amable shook his head. "How can you be so cool and in control so soon after coming around for the first time? The Weird room informed me about Twarbie. I know she's trying to be different."

Once this gets out.... "You can't let anyone know. The other winkles are horrible, and they'd kill her for sure. I mean they already were, but now if they know what you know—."

"It's okay."

"It is?" Alex sighed in relief.

"Well, no not exactly." Amable held a hand out to halt Alex's outburst. "First, I'm keeping what I know secret, from everyone. Second, well... the Weird thinks you'll handle the problems you've created—."

"Me! I—! Alex would've said more, but Amable cut him off.

"Alex, calm down or Gursha's going to kick me out of here. There's a reason Mrs. Soaley risked her life for you and two days ago, you proved some of the possibilities. You caused changes that no one would've thought possible...," Amable paused and then with a thoughtful expression continued, "except for perhaps the Weird. Before what you did, no one knew lepercauls could be anything but nasty, let alone heal other people like they did. And you've made a change with the winkles in just a few months. When I've been trying for years to change them. The worst of it is—." Amable coughed into one of his large hands. Then he ran a hand through his hair, sighing heavily. Amable's foot long tufts of hair drooped falling flat down the side of his neck and onto his chest. Next, he coughed again.

A couple of times Alex started to open his mouth to say something, but he stopped himself. *Is Amable ever going to finish telling me what the worst is?* At another sigh from Amable, Alex wanted to yank on those two tufts of hair. *Enough already.* Fortunately, someone else ran out of patience with Amable. With a lurch Amable stumbled against Alex. The holo-bed shifted slightly from the force. Behind Amable, Alex spotted an angry Gursha.

Amable looked over his shoulder. "Hey. That hurt."

Gursha grabbed Amable's hair tufts. "Of course, I'm a nurse and I know just where to kick for maximum pain. Now tell Alex what you need to tell him, or I'm going to yank on your tufts and we both know how much that hurts."

Amable turned back to Alex, and as he began to speak tears began to run down his face. "I didn't believe in you. I didn't provide help when the Weird told me too. As a result, the Weird says you probably should've died, but your cool resolve in danger and luck proved better than expected. I'm sorry."

Alex couldn't say anything. *I could've died.* Images of the many times he'd come close to dying and yet somehow managed not to flashed through his mind's eye.

Gursha's gentle words drew Alex from his memories. "Okay, Amable, you should get back to your office. I think you're overdue for your therapy."

Amable grinned, not quite his normal look, but close. "Yes. You're right. I can't let myself get maudlin. There's too much work to do."

Alex watched Amable turn and start across the clinic. It would be easy not to say anything, just let him leave. "Sir, Amable, it's okay. Just like you said when I was in the lepercaul wild. I'm just a teenager, who understands very little."

Amable's ear tufts drooped back down and he hurriedly left.

Alex looked to Gursha. "I thought that would make him feel better."

Gursha shook her head. "Oh, Alex. You are quite the boy, but there's a lot you don't know about. Amable's upset, because he knows the power of a teenager. As a teenager, he saved his people from deems."

"Wow. Really? That's great."

"At the same time, he also left his people drifting, in stasis, somewhere in the galaxy. It tears him apart. He keeps thinking of what he could've done different. It's driven him crazy."

"Amable's crazy?"

"Absolutely. For someone to create the Academy and start trying to rescue whole planets from deems, they would have to be crazy. Of course, you show signs of craziness too."

Alex paused. *Me, crazy?* He remembered the fear of going into the wild, the mind-numbing terror of the baby lepercauls, and diving into the giant. *Maybe I am a bit crazy, but I'd do it—.*

Gursha interrupted his thoughts. "I'd better let your friends in. They're trying to break the door down."

The door opened. In tumbled a mass of people. Most of them fell to the floor, but Zeghes soared about the room. "Good to see you, Alex. Are you well? I've been trying to be with you. Unfortunately, Gursha keeps telling me to go eat. I saw Amable crying in the passageway. What happened? That was quite the battle in the Hall of Flight."

As the rest of the group untangled, Alex recognized A'idah, Hheilea, and Hymeron. All of them talked at once. At first, Alex didn't try to make out what they said, instead his eyes went to the doorway looking for someone else. No one else stood there. Then his eyes caught a glimpse of Hheilea's face. A bright red area covered one cheek and most of her jaw.

She stood with her hands on her hips glaring at him. "— you listening to us? No one else is coming in. Gursha only let us come see you. She said you and a winkle teenager were the worst of the injuries. I've heard the winkle, Twar—, whatever her name, is going to be okay too. That's good, I guess."

Alex grinned. Others were talking, but he didn't pay attention. The music, Hheilea's music, played in his mind. *Even though Hheilea's upset about Twarbie, she's letting me know this.* Something about the music was different, muted. "What happened to your face?"

Hheilea reached up to the red mark. "I-."

A'idah slung an arm around Hheilea's shoulders and said, interrupting, "You should've seen Hhy and his brother. They came charging into the hall wearing these backpacks and carrying squirt—."

Hymeron stepped in front of them. "We had those guns from a prank. I filled the tanks with salt water and we went hunting babies. Hhy—."

A different voice interrupted. Amazement filled the words. "I saw him charging at me. He ignored everyone else. When a bouncing baby hit the kimley, his name is Hhy, right in the face. Oh, and I have a name now. I'm Giyf. Hhy just kept running at me, with a small baby latched onto his face."

Alex's friends moved aside and he could finally see the speaker. A foot-tall man with reddish-gold curly hair stood waving his arms as he continued saying, "I wouldn't have minded the idea of getting sprayed by salt water. I was eager to become an adult, but I had a meal inside which needed digesting. Then there was Helper. I didn't know why you jumped into me. It shocked me. I could feel you cutting at me and shoving inside. I'm glad you didn't hit any of my adult parts or I might be missing some pieces today. Although I guess a nurse could've fixed me. I still needed to figure out what to do with you. Seeing Hhy charging at me, while ignoring the pain of getting eaten and having you jump into me, made me suddenly understand what you meant about caring for others.

"Then you managed to shove the winkle out of me. All her, well I've been told not to repeat what she looked like. Some people find the description too gross, but somehow, she was still alive. It was terrible to see. I had a strange urge to help her. Those two babies who healed the old winkle ran up, held their hands out and a glow emanated from their hands. It surrounded the winkle and then faded. The winkle had stopped leaking fluids, but still didn't look good. Those babies called for help. At that moment, I realized what I could do for you. My skin split and I ejected you. Gursha tells me it was like giving you a second birth. She calls me your Godfather. I don't know what the term means, but I like it.

"You were in worse shape than the winkle, but with help from all of the babies we kept both of you alive, until the first nurse arrived to take over. I'm glad you have a nose, ears, and hair again. Hhy must really care for you. He knelt by you crying, as the fight was going on all around us. I had to get the baby off him. Then a big raptor, Ytell, arrived and took control of the situation."

The memory of the pain hit Alex like a sledge hammer. He shuddered. "Thanks, everyone. Gursha, how bad... I mean...."

Gursha stepped forward. "Okay, everyone, time to go. My patient needs to rest. Sorry, Zeghes, that goes for you too. Alex, don't think about the past, just rest."

~**********~

The next day Zeghes came to the clinic and waited for Gursha to let Alex go.

Finally, she said, "Now remember, no excitement. You might be feeling much better, but your nervous system is still recovering. Also, your AI is still offline. It took more damage for its size than you did. When it comes back online, you need to be gentle with it. It's going to have some emotional trauma to deal with. And make sure you don't forget to come back after your first class."

Just what I need, my own computer with emotional issues. "Okay, I've got to go. You heard Amable. He's held up my flock's classes, until I could rejoin them. We can't afford to fall behind."

After submitting to another four-armed hug, Alex made his escape. Zeghes nudged him with his beak. "I could give you a ride."

"I'll be fine, Zeghes. Where are we meeting the flock?" *I thought some of them would've come with Zeghes to get me.*

"We're having lunch together, and then we go to our first class."

Walking through many empty passageways, Alex said, "This is a big ship, but we haven't seen anyone. Where is everyone?"

"Uh..., busy. Everyone must be busy."

They turned a corner to see another long empty passageway, with a large opening at the far end. "Busy? Busy, everyone is busy doing something somewhere..." Alex paused. Terrible memories tugged at his mind. "Is that the Hall of Flight ahead of us?"

"Yes. Are you in shallow water?"

"Yeah. But I've got to go back there sometime. It might as well be now."

Zeghes led the way. After going through the opening he turned to look back. Alex followed, slowing down as he moved closer. The memory of the last time he entered the Hall of Flight came back. The baby had almost nibbled too much. *That's the past. I've got to move ahead. We haven't even reached the Academy yet. And then there's training followed by the test.* Squaring his shoulders, he forced himself to stride out more forcefully. Stepping through onto the balcony many things struck his awareness at once. A chanting rose from the hall. "Alex! Alex! Alex!"

His flock crowded around him, all congratulating him. Amable strode up to him. "In this great endeavor we're all a part of, there are moments like this, when we acknowledge the heroes amongst us."

Tears flowed down Alex's cheeks at the acclamation and he started shaking. *This is silly. I shouldn't cry.* But it was too much for him. Gursha hurried to his side with a flask. "Drink this. It'll help."

Gratefully, Alex drank the liquid. Immediately he did feel better. Looking up, he noticed his flock moving back from either side to give him a better view. Many people floated in bubbles. One in a closer bubble lifted a hand. Dizzy, Alex reached a hand out searching for stability. The person wore a brown robe with a caul pulled over her head. *It's Twarbie.* The girl drifted away into the vastness of the hall. His searching hand found a shoulder. He looked down to see Hheilea. The muted music gently lulled his mind.

"Are you okay?"

"Yeah..., I'm fine."

Hheilea said, "Let's get you down to the floor. Come share my bubble."

Alex nodded and joined her in a circle. *What's up with the music? It's changed.* Tingling traveling up his body briefly reminded him of his first experience with a bubble transport, but the immediacy of the muted music shunted that memory aside. Another thought rattled him. *The dance. Isn't the dance supposed to restart when I'm with Hheilea?* As their bubble lifted up, Alex started to speak, but then realized they only had partial privacy. *AI, contact Hheilea.* Nothing responded and then he remembered his AI was still offline. They had started to drift toward the tables down below. *Didn't Ytell say something about normal bubbles, and anyone can control them?* Alex leaned forward and willed the bubble to speed off toward an empty area of air in the great hall. He said, with a bit of urgency, "Hheilea, what's up with the music? It's different." And then stuttering with desperation, "And, and,

and how can we be together without the T'wasn't-to-be-is Dance starting again?"

"It's okay. Calm down."

Calm down? Ahhh.

Hheilea pulled on a chain around her neck and a green crystal slipped from under her shirt. "Hymeron gave me this. He told me not to ask who he got it from. Someday his secret dealings with all his contacts are going to get him into really big trouble. But this thing is really useful. And my dad gave me his approval, both for this crystal and for the T'wasn't-to-be-is Dance. Although, he's been crying a lot the last couple of days."

Hheilea shrugged. "He must be upset about me growing up. Although, a week ago he bubbled over with excitement, when he told me my T'wasn't-to-be-is would start soon. I really don't understand adults."

Then she grinned and almost squealed in excitement. "And soon we'll be adults. I can hardly wait. Except, I will. Hymeron's helped me realize it's not fair for you getting tossed into the T'wasn't-to-be-is. I mean, I've known about it for most of my life and was frightened and upset about it for the last few years. Now, I'm really excited and happy, but I can wait a couple of months before we become one. You need to be able to accept what we're going to have on your own terms."

Suddenly Hheilea grabbed Alex in a hug and turned her face up to his. Waves of the music assaulted him, as the music struggled to get louder.

Is she going to kiss me? Will the dance start? He shoved her away, breaking the hug. "Hheilea, there's all these people about. Control yourself."

Breathing hard, he aimed the bubble back at everyone else. *Wait a couple of months before we become one? She's crazy. I'm only fifteen. No way.* Below, he could see tables spread out and creatures of all kinds. At the end of the ride A'idah waited to grasp him by the arm. "About time you got here. What took you two so long? Come on, Alex, let me take you to the food. Hhy, you and Hymeron should eat with us."

Alex let A'idah lead him to the food. Flashes of a different time, suffering and frantic choices surfaced to be overrun by the cheer around him. Wonderful smells began to make his mouth water. "What's that smell? It's wonderful."

Hymeron laughed, and then said, "I thought you would remember it. That's lillyputi dessert. Because of how humans react, it's now on the restricted list for all of you. Now if you eat it, there's something in it which will make you violently ill, in other words... vomit. So, I... advise you to stay away from it."

The smell pulled Alex's eyes to a table where he recognized Giyf. The lepercaul was dressed in a green suit, which went really well with his short reddish-gold hair. He held a spoon loaded with lillyputi dessert and moaned. "This is the worst thing about being an adult. The food tastes so much better, but I can only eat a little before my stomach hurts."

Alex wanted to tell Giyf to eat some of the dessert for him. *That would be cruel. He already wants to eat more. I could just stand here and enjoy the smell.*

"Hey, Alex, come over here and try pompadodies."

Looking around, Alex finally recognized the speaker. Ekbal stood at a nearby table with bowls heaped with small round balls of varying colors. "What are pompadodies?"

"They're something the dwarves came up with to make up for humans not getting to enjoy lillyputi anymore. Each ball is different."

Alex shrugged and started making his way over to Ekbal. "Okay. I'll give it a try."

"Here, try this one," Ekbal held out one of the balls to Alex. "Just let it sit in your mouth for a second and then bite into it." Ekbal watched as his flock-mate tried the food.

The small ball was about as big around as the end of Alex's thumb. Its texture in his hand was rough, but in his mouth felt very pleasant. A clean taste swept his mouth. *Wow. It's like I just got my teeth brushed.* Just before he bit into it, Alex remembered Ekbal liked hot-spicy foods. *Oh well, here goes nothing.* Biting down brought an explosion of flavor which quickly faded as the morsel melted away and he swallowed. *Chocolate with a hint of citrus?* "I want to try another." The next was just the same except for the flavor. *Coffee?* "These are amazing. The flavor is there for just a moment and then it's gone."

Nodding and grinning, Ekbal said, "Somehow the food chooses a flavor you really like the first few times, and then starts getting more random the more you eat." He popped another into his mouth. "Ew, that one tasted like something which died a week ago. I guess they're designed that way to keep it from being addictive. No one wants to keep eating them once the flavors get too unpredictable."

"Hello, Alex" A voice said from over his head.

Alex looked up to see Ytell. "Ytell, it's great to see you again."

"Likewise. I'm glad you finished the training and survived dealing with the lepercauls and winkles. I would've been to see you in the clinic, but I used the last few days to do some more planning of all your upcoming training. Soon we reach the Academy, and there'll be little time for anything but studying and going to classes. Remember, your professors are aliens, and it might be interesting at times dealing with how different they are from you Earthlings. After you eat, I'll be gathering the flock to take you to your first class. Enjoy the food."

Alex said, "Thanks." *I'm looking forward to classes and studying after all the excitement I've had.* Above the raptor's head, Alex caught sight of a figure floating in a bubble. The person wore a brown robe. With one hand the person threw her caul back revealing her face and hair. It was Twarbie. She waved and Alex waved back. *Wait. What's she doing waving at me?* He remembered her words about the danger in being a friend and then about Amable saying something about the winkles changing. *Does that mean..., we can be friends... or... How am I going to concentrate on my classes? Somehow, I've got to be sure we Earthlings pass our test at the end of the year.*

TLW Savage, Author

Tim lives in his RV and is now an Idahoan. He's actually Tim Walker. Savage is an old family name, and he decided to start using it to make it easier for fans to differentiate him from other authors.

A grandpa, he and his wife enjoy their children and grandchildren. He loves making great food and gets even more enjoyment from watching family and friends eat the food.

He began creating stories at an early age. One night his seven-year-old sister woke screaming, and he went to comfort her. On the spur of the moment, the twelve-year-old Tim created a fantastical story for her, calming her with attention grabbing details. He still remembers that story. Tim has an even earlier memory of creating a story sometime between six and seven-years-old, but he doesn't remember much of that incident.

Tim has one more book he's working on for this series. It's called Alex and the Crystal of Jedh. Next, he's working on four other books in the same story line. They will be set back on Earth. He's going to explore the location, a remote mountain range called Henry's mountains in south-eastern Utah. They are a fascinating place with many interesting plants and animals. The geology is unique. He'll be going back to Henry's mountains a number of times to get the details of those stories right.

Tim's fascinated by everything from flowers to Genghis Kahn and sand to Mount Everest. He finds people particularly interesting and is always on the watch for interesting features and personality quirks. If you come to his website and visit, you might find yourself in a book. He's active in local writing groups and is a beta reader for other writers. You can find him at:

tlwalkerauthor.com   or   his   new   website tlwsavageauthor.com

Contact the Author

I would love to hear back from my fans. Please contact me at my email: tlwalker@twalkerauthor.com. Plus, if you provide me with a suggestion, such as a type of animal or a scene, and I use it, I will then include your name on the acknowledgment page. Also, for my younger fans if you take the book to school and your whole class makes a suggestion and I use it, then I will include the whole class, everyone's name, on a special page just for them. Remember the simpler the suggestion the easier and more likely I will use it. Thanks for being a fan. I hope to see you someday at a book signing.

Author Visit

Tim has started doing author visits at schools. He loves doing them and wants to do more. Contact his agent Laura Barr at (360) 584-4241, email laurambarr91@gmail.com.

Made in the USA
Middletown, DE
06 May 2019